BRIEF ENCOUNTERS
A TALENT FOR TALES
Edited by
ALLISON JONES
New
Fiction

New Fiction
First published in Great Britain in 2010 by:
New Fiction
Remus House
Coltsfoot Drive
Peterborough
PE2 9JX
Telephone: 01733 890099
Website: www.forwardpress.co.uk

SB ISBN 978-1-84418-533-7

FOREWORD

Forward Press was established in 1989 in order to provide a bridge to publication for unknown poets and authors. We firmly believe that creative writing should be an opportunity open to all, no matter their background or academic experience. As a result we are proud that over the years we have been able to allow thousands of writers the chance to see their work in print.

The contributions from our fantastic writers are always a joy to read and there is sure to be something for everyone within this, our latest anthology. We hope you agree that this collection is one that will inspire and entertain again and again.

CONTENTS

THE STORIES

ESCAPE INTO THE NIGHT

Olive Tate

Jamie, a twelve-year-old schoolboy, lives with his mother and father in the East End of London. He loves his little dog Skippy, having found her in an old sack, securely tied and dumped in a river to drown. He trains Skippy with help from his father, Crane. Jamie and Crane often talk about owning training kennels together, but Crane is a notorious gambler and is sometimes in trouble with the police. He has an ugly scar down one side of his face, which is a knife wound he received whilst found cheating at a card game in Ireland.

One day Crane tells his wife Jean and Jamie that he has to travel to Ireland which will be for the last time. Jamie wants to go, but is told he must stay and look after his mother.

After supper one evening, Jamie is sitting in his bedroom with Skippy looking at a photo of his father and a little map of Ireland, pinpointing Killorgin, where Puck Fair is held every year in August, always attracting gypsies, thieves and gamblers, and where Crane is well known.

The following morning Jamie decides to play truant from school, knowing his mother will be at work in the factory. He can then take Skippy and a few belongings, having in mind to go to Ireland to find his father and bring him home, so leaves a note for his mother explaining his intentions and telling her not to worry.

Having passed a particular café often on his way to school, he notices and remembers removal vans displaying signs saying, Long distance removals - Ireland to England, and hopefully meaning they would be empty travelling back to Ireland.

On arriving at the parking area for the removal vans, with Skippy tucked firmly under his arm, Jamie tries the door of the first van and, finding it to be locked, tries the second and, to his surprise, it opens, allowing him to climb inside, where he can see many wooden crates containing straw and paper, obviously for breakable articles when being transported. On hearing footsteps coming towards the van, Jamie, still clutching Skippy, quickly jumps into one of the crates and covers himself and Skippy with straw. Jamie realises it's the driver as the van begins to move.

Arriving safely in Ireland, the driver stops at a petrol station to fill up and make a lengthy phone call at a kiosk, thus allowing Jamie and Skippy to escape into the night.

After what seems like many hours of walking, they approach a large tree trunk and, feeling exhausted, Jamie sits on it, joined by Skippy who suddenly jumps up and starts to sniff the air. Jamie is rather frightened and wonders what is out there, so he stands up on the tree trunk, where he can see what looks like a campfire, and the smell of cooking is almost unbearable! They approach and can see an old man sitting round the fire, tucking into food from a Billy can, not noticing the intruders, until Skippy barks at him, making him drop the food on the ground, which she quickly devours, leaving Jamie to come face to face with a shotgun! The old man always has this near at hand in case he is approached by thieves, as he is known to carry a lot of money in his haversack, which he makes from his poaching career. Jamie apologises, and on realising he is a harmless young boy, the old man offers him food. Sitting round the campfire, the old man says his name is Sam and asks why a young boy is out late at night with his little dog. Telling Sam his name is Jamie and he is on his way to Puck Fair to find his father, he shows Sam a photo of Crane who the old man recognises as Scar Face, and tells Jamie that his father will be at the fair somewhere, playing cards.

One evening after supper, sitting around the campfire listening to Sam's harmonica playing for their evening entertainment, which makes Skippy howl and Jamie sing like a choirboy with a sore throat, Sam tells Jamie he will be getting up early the next day, as misty mornings are good for rabbit shoots. Jamie says to Sam, 'Look after Skippy for me, won't you?'

To which Sam replies, 'You know I will. I love that little dog!'

A little later, as Sam stands ready and waiting to shoot the next moving object in his shotgun sights, his vision is slightly blurred by the rising sun shining in his eyes. However, whilst waiting for Sam, Skippy sees a rabbit in the opposite direction which she cannot resist to chase, but it is too quick for her and scampers out of sight. As Skippy makes her way back to Sam from a different direction, leaping and bounding in the long grass, she arrives in Sam's shotgun sights, and thinking it is a rabbit, he fires. He walks towards the object, which he has just shot, sees something wriggling and can hear whimpering. To his horror he realises it to be Skippy and bends down to stroke her as she lifts her head and looks up at him, gives another little whimper and lies back and dies. Picking her up, Sam carefully places Skippy in some bushes and covers her up with his old coat. He is devastated by what he has done and with tears rolling down his weather-beaten old face, and with drooping head, he shuffles back to camp to tell Jamie what has happened. Jamie, seeing Sam approaching, calls out, 'I've got breakfast ready for you and Skippy.' As Sam slowly walks to his seat, which is an old bucket turned upside down, he puts his face in his hands and, crying like a baby, manages to tell Jamie he has mistakenly shot Skippy for a rabbit. Jamie tries to be brave but is very tearful, and after a while they return to where Sam has placed Skippy in the bushes. Here they make a grave by scraping the earth away with their bare hands, placing Skippy in it, still covered with Sam's old coat. They cover the grave with earth, and Sam places his rifle for a headstone, knowing his poaching days are over, as he can't face up to firing a shotgun again.

Jamie is broken-hearted having to bury Skippy and tells Sam he cannot go on without her and wants to go home. Sam understands and says he will escort him back home to his mother, and passing back through the woods where they first met, he tells Jamie he has lots of money buried in several places which will pay for their return journey to England.

Arriving safely in England, Jamie and Sam say goodbye to each other, both with tears in their eyes, and Sam, slowly walking away, turns round to wave and disappears for the long journey back to Ireland to find Crane and tell him what has happened.

After accidentally shooting Skippy, Sam's thoughts return to the late summer evening when a 'would be' intruder tried to attack him, not knowing Skippy was nearby, lying on Sam's old fishing coat. Jamie was down by the stream collecting water in the Billy can to brew for a cup of tea and for cooking supper.

Sam was sitting on his usual seat, an old upturned black bucket, listening to the evening chorus of so many different birds singing and twittering, and looking up to the sky admiring the moon and stars, which always seem to attract him, as he is a real old country loving person. Sam does not need a lot of money, only enough for cartridges and his shotgun and a meal of fish and chips when visiting local country shows as he travels the country on his way to Puck Fair.

Unfortunately, Sam did not know there was an intruder lurking by with a keen eye on his haversack, in which many gypsies and thieves knew he kept money from his poaching career. Jumping from behind Sam, the thief tried to steal the haversack, but Skippy immediately went to the rescue, attacking him and biting his leg really hard with a vice like grip, making him yell and startling Sam, who also went onto the attack with his fists hitting the intruder's jaw, with Skippy still hanging on to the man's trouser leg, with lots of growling. The thief managed to break free and run off, hotly pursued by Skippy, until Sam called her back, making a great fuss of her and saying what a good girl she was.

Jamie, returning from the stream, wondered what all the noise was about, which he could hear down by the stream. Sam told Jamie that Skippy had attacked an intruder and chased him away so she would be presented with a tasty supper and extra rations!

This episode is often in Sam's thoughts, especially after sadly shooting and killing Skippy, which has devastated him.

After several weeks of travelling, Puck Fair is now in sight and Sam, not recovering from the shock of shooting Skippy, often feels tired and ill.

It is late evening when he arrives feeling tired and hungry, but the lights of the fairground and cheery music give out a warm glowing atmosphere. The smell of fish and chips and burger bars fills the night air, with mouth-watering results as Sam searches in his pockets for some money, finding enough to buy some fish and chips.

After eating and having renewed energy for walking around the fairground, Sam is now excited, with the feeling that he will meet Crane soon, probably in one of the beer tents. After looking in several tents and feeling a little disappointed, Sam spies a cleverly hidden tent amongst the tall trees in the wooded area, with a large notice displayed at the entrance saying, Strictly no entry - card game in progress - keep out, giving the feeling something serious is taking place. Sam is really excited now and cautiously creeps through the tent flap and stands motionless behind the card table, unnoticed by the serious-looking men, who do not take their eyes from the cards. A typical looking gambling scene is in progress, with scruffy-looking men, some wearing gold rings and necklaces and others with white, red and blue spotted chokers tied around their necks. Several glasses of whiskey and beer are to be seen on the card table, and present is the unmistakable man with the ugly scar on his face, Jamie's father!

Little arguments that have been brewing all evening suddenly turn into a noisy brawl, attracting men from the nearby tents, who all like a good punch-up, just for the fun of it! Sam is thoroughly enjoying the atmosphere and is reminded of his younger days when he was involved in many punch-ups. There are several glasses of beer miraculously still standing on the card table, but only one is still full to the top, which Sam reaches for and drinks quickly, as it is thirsty work watching a punch-up. Then suddenly Sam sees Crane being attacked by several men, with one grabbing him by the throat and almost choking him. Sam goes in to help Crane and, punching their way free, Sam calls out to him, 'Come on, let's get out of here. I have got a lot to tell you.'

After a long conversation, and hearing about how Sam accidentally shot Skippy, Crane decides to return home and, realising that Sam is an old man without a poaching career or home, he invites him to England to start a new venture with Jamie and the family with their training kennels. Sam then explains to Crane about his buried money, which they retrieve on the way home, and says he would like to invest this into the new training kennels.

As they leave the fairground in a van which Crane had parked nearby, he notices two puppies in a crate by the beer tent, with a For Sale sign saying, £5 each. As both dogs look just like Skippy, Crane tells Sam to stay put, hastily jumps from the van with a view to buying the pups, and excitedly calls to Sam, 'This is the beginning of our new training establishment!'

Telephoning home from a nearby telephone kiosk, Crane tells Jamie he is on his way home with Sam, who saved his life during a big fight, and also that Sam will be living with them as a manager in their new training establishment. He also tells Jamie that he has a wonderful surprise for him and will see him in a couple of days. Jamie tells Jean the news of his father and that he will be home in two days. She has recovered from her short illness and is excited about the new kennels, as she always felt it could be a lifesaver for Crane from his violent career.

The Reunion

Jamie and his mother have just finished fixing a banner over the front door, which reads Welcome home Dad and Sam, with Jamie not knowing there are two puppies around the corner in Crane's van, which he has parked just out of sight from the house.

Crane and Sam jump out with the two puppies, only to meet Jean and Jamie waiting at the front gate for them. After lots of tears, hugs and kisses to and from the family, Jamie is almost hysterical with delight now, as he gently takes one of the puppies in his arms, with his father saying, 'That was the surprise I had for you, Jamie.' With that, his son repeats the name, 'Skippy, Skippy!' and puts baby Skippy carefully on the ground just as the other puppy runs to join them. Jamie is so joyfully happy having two puppies and his father and Sam at home. Once again, they all embrace and enter the house, where Crane tells the family he is home for good and Puck Fair and gambling are only memories, with the dream of training kennels now to become a reality. Jean also has tears of happiness and now feels that her husband will be here in the future, especially when Crane tells her that Sam has invested enough money for a deposit for their training kennels, with Sam to be the manager.

Jean makes her way to the table where there is a pile of magazines, which she has collected from time to time, with one in which she has underlined 'Country house and training kennels for sale amongst beautiful scenery'.

Later the next day, the family and Sam visit the kennels to find that they are just what they have always dreamed of, with enough room for boarding kennels, and plenty of ground for training the owners and their dogs.

Subsequently, arrangements are made to purchase the kennels, with a view to move in as quickly as possible, with no regrets at leaving the East End of London for the country.

Sam suggests that a big sign be placed at the entrance to the drive leading to the house and kennels reading, Skippy Training and Boarding Kennels, with a little drawing underneath of the two Skippy dogs, which is happily accepted by the family, who are now all looking forward to a new life!

A DAY AT THE SEASIDE

Philip Herriman

It was summer - Bognor Regis - not exactly what you might call high summer, but high enough to encourage holidaymakers onto the beach. Mr Pettigrew joined them with his towel and beach mat, the bag and a sense of duty. He wasn't there to enjoy himself.

Two weeks ago they'd cremated his father. It had rained in the inconsiderate way of the British weather. His father would have understood. He wasn't a man who'd expected much, and had been rewarded accordingly. He reminded Mr Pettigrew of a worn-out carpet they once had in the front room, which had been rolled up and put on the fire.

Mr Pettigrew held the bag tightly.

He pictured his father on their annual holiday gazing wistfully out to sea. As a child he'd wondered what his father was looking at. But as he grew older, and knew his mother better, he understood. Now his father was dead, worn out by a marriage which had promised little and offered less. The marriage service should have been a warning - for richer or poorer; for better, for worse.

Mr Pettigrew senior had only achieved the second part of either.

But he had enjoyed the seaside.

As he lay in bed he'd gripped his son's hand. 'We had some good times didn't we lad - at the seaside. When I'm gone throw this in the sea for me.' He pressed a pebble into Mr Pettigrew's hand. 'I brought one back for every year.'

Mr Pettigrew remembered the pile of pebbles in the back garden with the Union Jack on top - like a Buddhist prayer flag carrying the dreams of the elder Mr Pettigrew to a land where his wife couldn't reach him.

'Your mother won't let my ashes be thrown on't sea. She wants me here where she can keep an eye on me.'

Mr Pettigrew had seen the urn on the breakfast table where his father used to sit, next to the milk jug and the muesli.

'No need to tell your mother. She wouldn't understand.'

It was his last small act of defiance.

Mr Pettigrew felt he too was taking part in that act of defiance against his mother. He'd even gone a step further. Creeping downstairs late one night he'd poured his father's ashes into a lemonade bottle, replacing the remains with a mixture of muesli and ashes from the living room fire.

The following morning he announced he was going out for the day. His mother said nothing. Mr Pettigrew had noticed since his father's death she had become a shadow of her former self. He'd left her gazing at the urn, as if willing it to speak so she could shout at it.

Now he held the pebble, recalling the moment it had been left in his hand as his father slipped away - passing on the baton as it were to the next generation.

The bottle was in the bag.

Mr Pettigrew donned his bathing costume as he had when a child, with the awkward actions of a three-legged giraffe, and lay down in the warm sun. Suddenly he was aware of a noise by his left ear. Looking up he saw a large herring gull pecking at the lemonade bottle which had rolled out of the bag, some of his father already mingling with the sand.

Without thinking, he shouted loudly, 'Leave my father alone.'

A family of four looked at him oddly, and moved away.

Grasping the first thing that came to hand - in this case a toffee, which he'd been about to eat, he threw it at the seagull - and missed. The seagull pursued the toffee and impaled it. It flapped around plaintively in the sand, mewing in a strangulated way with the toffee stuck to the end of its beak.

Mr Pettigrew ignored it, and holding his father's pebble in one hand and the lemonade bottle in the other, wove his way among the basking crowd into the sea.

'Come on Dad,' he said.

He was followed by a small black dog who had watched Mr Pettigrew feeding the seagull and was hoping for similar largesse. Mr Pettigrew waded out until he was waist high, beyond most of the swimmers, and began to unscrew the top of the lemonade bottle. Behind him, swimming and unnoticed, the small black terrier followed the thin trail of ashes from the punctured lemonade bottle. Before Mr Pettigrew could release his father on an unsuspecting ocean, the dog seized his chance - and the bottle - in his teeth, and attempted to make off with it.

They fought as the summer sun danced on the water, and more and more of Mr Pettigrew's father dappled the sea. Mr Pettigrew's task was the more difficult. He'd fallen into a gully between two sandbars and kept sinking, while the black terrier had secured a firmer footing on the sandbar. To the casual observer it must have seemed that either Mr Pettigrew was very small or the dog had very long legs. Finally Mr Pettigrew fell upon the dog and wrestled it into submission, securing what was left of his father's remains. The dog began to howl.

Mr Pettigrew unscrewed the top and shook the contents of the bottle into the air, but the wind and current were against him. Instead of being carried out to sea on the wind, Mr Pettigrew senior descended on his son, and enveloped him in a cloud of ash. Mr Pettigrew wiped his eyes. The sea was covered in a film of ash, and the dog had developed a moustache as it savaged the empty lemonade bottle on the incoming tide.

Released from his combat with the dog, Mr Pettigrew completed his promise to his father. Pulling his arm back, he threw the pebble high into the summer sky. The little dog watched as the pebble of dreams described a glinting parabola in the sunshine, and plopped into the sea.

Then with an excited bark it launched itself into the deep water and made off toward the French coast. Mr Pettigrew watched it for a moment, turned and made his way back to the beach.

As he reached the beach he heard a small boy wailing.

'Where's Blackie?' he shrieked. 'My doggy's been drownded. I seen that man do it.' He pointed at Mr Pettigrew.

The boy was joined by his angry parents. 'Where's our Wayne's dog? He says you drowned it.'

'He was talking about his father earlier,' someone else said. 'What have you done with him?'

'I threw him into the sea,' said Mr Pettigrew.

It was not a sensible thing to say.

'He's drowned his poor old dad too.'

A beleaguered Mr Pettigrew, hemmed in by a semicircle of people on the edge of the water, tried to explain.

Suddenly a shout went up. 'There he is.'

'Is it his dad?'

'No. It's the dog. There. Over there.'

In the distance where the waves were breaking over some rocks a small black head was swimming in circles trying to locate the pebble.

'You go and get Blackie,' Wayne's father said menacingly. 'It's your fault he's there.'

He edged Mr Pettigrew into the water.

There was nothing for it - and the man was bigger than him. He made his way half wading and half swimming towards the enthusiastic mongrel which was yapping furiously at something on the rock.

Mr Pettigrew was not a strong swimmer and, by the time he reached the dog, he was exhausted. He picked it up and clambered onto the rock. There was a cheer from the beach.

Suddenly he was aware of a presence. They were not alone. Turning he was confronted by the baleful stare of a seagull - with a toffee stuck to its beak. There was mutual recognition. The bird advanced menacingly. But it hadn't seen Blackie who sprang from Mr Pettigrew's lap and hurled himself at the toffee. Taken by surprise the seagull opened its beak sharply and the toffee fell to the victor. Mr Pettigrew fell into the sea, followed by Blackie who landed on his head. Mr Pettigrew emerged from the waves wearing the dog like a bedraggled busby.

Back on the beach the babble of voices was stilled by Wayne's mother shrieking, 'Wayne. Where's our Wayne?'

And there he was swimming out to rescue his pet. Mr Pettigrew was horrified. With the tide, coming in fast, the small boy would be cut off. He plunged into the water and, half walking and half swimming fought his way towards the boy. As he reached Wayne, the dog once again scrambled onto his head and Mr Pettigrew sank. At the same time Wayne secured a footing on the sandbar. He pulled Mr Pettigrew to safety. Together they made for the shore, Mr Pettigrew in the lead, holding Wayne by the hand the dog barking furiously. Above them the seagull wheeled in the sky screaming abuse and dive bombing Mr Pettigrew like a kamikaze pilot.

To the onlookers it seemed that Mr Pettigrew had pushed Wayne to safety on the sandbar, and he was hailed a hero. Someone had explained about the ashes in the lemonade bottle. Wayne's father was apologetic. Mrs Wayne was effusive and kissed Mr Pettigrew, perhaps a little too enthusiastically, her husband thought.

'Your dad would have been right proud of you,' she said.

A tear came into Mr Pettigrew's eye.

He hoped his father had enjoyed his last day at the seaside.

CLAUDE AND WILL

Jenny Bosworth

Claude my husband of fifty-six years had died peacefully. He had simply stopped breathing. Two days ago he was reading the paper in the room while I was cooking dinner. When I went to fetch him for dinner his face was twisted and one arm was limp. My poor Claude had suffered a stroke.

I had been vigil at his bedside at hospital ever since. After a weep and a very sweet cup of tea for shock I took a taxi home from hospital. As a rule I'm quite chatty to the taxi drivers, but not today. Well they would not expect me to when my beloved Claude had just passed away.

Arriving home from hospital I made myself a coffee. I supposed I should let people know but I just could not face it. Most of the neighbours would be out at work so they would not be bothering me. Stan from number forty-six would be upset. You would think they were arch enemies the way they would argue about football but they were the best of mates really.

Married in wartime, Claude and me, known each other six months. Dad didn't want me to marry him, said it would not last, and it would all end in tears. We had a happy marriage though no children, which I was disappointed about. I would have liked a daughter to confide in. Claude used to say that the secret of a good marriage was being able to admit when you were wrong and I think he practised what he preached.

I remember our wedding day as if it was yesterday. Wartime, could not afford much, not that there was much to have in the war. Don't have a picture because nobody had a camera. Claude could not afford a wedding ring for me so he used a curtain ring. He bought me a beautiful ring about ten years later. Won a thousand pounds on the pools did my Claude, so he wanted to spoil me. Loved sport did Claude, watching it I mean, always reckoned he was too lazy to play.

Proposed to me at a sporting event. The village cricket match. He got down on one knee.

'Will you marry me Alice?'

'Claude,' I muttered, 'everyone is looking.'

'Will you marry me?' repeated Claude even louder.

'Yes,' I answered, flinging my arms round him and kissing him, 'sorry.'

'For what?'

'For kissing you in a public place.'

I could have crept into a hole and people were clapping. I'm not sure whether it was the cricket or us they were clapping. Claude was not much for going out but he would take me to sporting events. Went to the test match at Lords twice. I have even spoken to Geoffrey Boycott. Forgot to get his autograph, silly me.

My thoughts were stopped by the telephone ringing. I could have done without it but thought I had better answer it.

It was my friend Irene who lives two streets away. Went to school with her. Forever in trouble at school she was. Anyway she rang to see how Claude was.

'He has died,' I told her. 'Just stopped breathing, very peacefully he went.'

Irene was very sorry and offered to come round. I said there was no need. When I had put the phone down I wondered whether to ring round people and tell them. After a long debate with myself I decided to. Would you believe I rang thirty people? My two sisters, my brother and his wife, and others that would be at home in the daytime.

Then I suddenly realised I would have to see about Claude's funeral. I was just about to ring the undertakers when the doorbell rang. Who's that? I thought. Only one way to find out, answer it. On doing so there was a man standing there with a big bunch of flowers.

'Hello,' I greeted.

'Some flowers for you love.'

'Oh, they are nice,' I answered.

They were from Irene. Not used to getting flowers me. Claude never once bought me flowers, not even on my birthday. Had a job remembering his own birthday, let alone mine. Could not see the point of celebrating getting a year older.

'Don't I know you from somewhere?' asked the man.

'I seem to know your face,' I said, trying to think.

'Alice,' he almost shouted.

'Pardon!'

'You're Alice Forman.'

'Used to be, who are you?'

'Will Dochett.'

'Will Dochett,' I repeated, none the wiser.

'We used to go out together Alice.'

'Oh Will,' I shouted, 'that was years ago.'

'About forty, I'd say.'

'Come in for a minute.'

As soon as I said that I felt guilty about it. Having a man in the house when poor Claude had just died.

'Forgive me Claude,' I muttered.

'Pardon?'

'Nothing,' I answered.

Will and I courted for about a year. Then his family moved away and he had to go with them. Farmers they were and proud of it. Will still had that twinkle in his eye.

'Like a cuppa?' I asked.

'Yes please.'

'What are you doing bringing flowers round?'

'Stopping at my son's next door to your friend's, and she asked me to bring them.'

'You're married then?' I asked, putting the kettle on.

'Wife died three years ago, cancer you know.'

'Claude, my husband, died this morning.'

'Oh dear, I'm sorry to hear that.'

'He had a stroke and just stopped breathing. Pleased he went peacefully.'

'That is the main thing. Miss them though, I still miss my wife, suppose I always will. How about we go out for a meal for old time's sake?'

That was Will. Claude had just died and he wanted to go celebrating. Had not the tact to think of my feelings. Reckon that is men for you.

'I have a funeral to arrange,' I snapped, 'I have not rung the funeral directors yet.'

'Well tomorrow night then.'

'What will people think with my Claude not cold in his coffin?'

Will eventually persuaded me. I felt it was wrong to go and kept begging Claude's forgiveness. Will and I talked of where we went when we were courting. A ballroom called Sunlight was a favourite place. Got quite good at the waltz me.

Next day he went home fifty miles away. Did not even tell me he was going. Found out from Irene. The next few months were hard for me. Grieving for Claude and getting used to life without him.

Night-times were worst. I would weep for Claude. Sometimes I thought of getting in touch with Will, but felt it was wrong. Claude had only just died. It was too soon to start a relationship. But Will would cheer me up.

One day I was in the town about six months later and I ran into Irene.

'Will's back in town,' she informed me.

'Will?' I replied.

'The gentleman that bought the flowers.'

'Oh him,' I said pretending not to care.

In a way I was hurt that he had not been in touch. I wished I had asked Irene how long he had been in town and why. A fortnight passed and still I had not heard from him so I decided to forget all about Will. About a week later there was a knock on the door early in the evening. When I answered it Will was standing there.

'Will!' I shouted.

'Alice.'

I invited him in and he told me he had moved down here. I was still thinking maybe I should not have anything to do with him but I could not help myself. We started going out and I got to know the waltz again.

'I have never been so happy since Betsy died,' said Will one day.

'I'm happy too, and I'm sure Claude would want me to be,' I smiled.

We hugged and kissed, even though there were people watching.

'I've come to be near my family,' he told me.

'Where do you live?'

'In a bungalow two streets away,' he smiled. 'Felt I wanted my family around.'

Will had a son Joe who was a bricklayer, his wife Anne and two beautiful daughters, Joanne who was twelve and Maizie who was eight. He took me to have dinner with them and I was so nervous, silly me. No need to be at all. They were so nice. Don't know what they thought about me latching on to their dad when I had lost Claude not long previously.

'They loved you,' Will told me afterwards, putting his arms round me and kissing me.

'Well I loved them,' I replied kissing him back.

I did lay awake wondering whether I should finish with Will. It did not seem fair on Claude. As Irene said, 'Claude has gone and he would want you to be happy.'

Now I am putting on my blue suit to marry Will a year after Claude's passing. I think we will be happy until one of us stops breathing.

THE SYNOPSIS OF A PARTING

A story without gender

Ron Vickerson

It's one of those dark, dank, cold English kind of days. As I walk, my breath escapes from my mouth and floats tantalisingly in front of me mingling into the damp grey mist of the early morning. Tangible eerie spiders' webs seem to hang from every tree and lamp post just waiting to trail sticky webs across one's face. They make me shiver. The pavement seems to be covered with glutinous black slime. People hurry past, their heads down adamantly refusing to make eye contact. They are afraid that I may smile in their direction and expect them to return it. Their hands are pushed deeply into the pockets of dark voluminous coats. Collars are turned up tightly around their necks. Faces pinched and white, except for the tips of bright red noses peering over the edges of long fringed scarves.

This station is really depressing. One suspects that it was built complete with dirt and grime embedded in the dark grey stone and designed to be forever cold.

There seems to be a lot of people milling around the platform. I can pick out the would-be passengers from those who have only come to say goodbye. Some are seemingly concerned and weepy-eyed, whilst others obviously just can't wait to get away. There are quite a few standing amongst the crowd clutching their tickets tightly. The wonderment on their faces suggests to me that they have never travelled on a train before and cannot decide whether to stay or run away whilst they still have the chance. There are others whose eyes betray their deepest feelings. Automatically my mind plans suitable treatments.

Don't wonder, keep your mind on the reason you are here.

The noise of screaming children shocks me out of my reverie. Wide-eyed children running and jumping have ventured too near the hypnotic edge of the platform. Their parents are calling them and will no doubt punish them to salve their own guilty feelings of neglect.

The train is late. A lot of passengers are striding irritably about the platform looking at their watches constantly checking them with the large white-faced station clock, with its loud tick and jerky arms. They won't make the train come any quicker.

As usual we are standing apart from the main crush. In awkward silence. Those shielded eyes make intense sidelong looks at me full of unspoken questions. Neither of us dares to break the silence, to utter the first word. Despite hugging my coat around me I am shivering. Oh God a nerve in my right eyelid is starting to twitch. I cannot stop fidgeting. I am aware that I am staring around and continually touching my nose and mouth with uncontrollable hands, I must seem to be an utter fool restlessly shifting my weight from one foot to the other. I wish the bloody train would come. I can't stand much more of those moist deep brown eyes searching my face, asking the questions that my eyes are begging will not be asked. Although I thought we had said all there was to stay last night I realise now that there are many questions that should be answered. I can read them in that sad pale face.

God I feel full of guilt. I am aware that panic is taking over, I feel as if I am about to be imprisoned and desperately need to find a way of escape. Don't panic. The train is here, the noise it makes as it roars into the station will have blotted out any words that I might have said. Now the voice that not long ago whispered soft words into my ears, now berates me in a loud voice. It's almost too much to bear.

The tirade continues as people begin to crowd around carriage doors jostling each other to ensure a good seat. It will soon be over, everything will be fine.

That look is breaking my heart. I have to be strong. I must persist, it will be best for both of us in the long run. I did try to explain that last night.

I should board the train. I don't want to leave time for conversation to develop yet I don't want to appear too eager to leave. I'll just pick up my case, it's not that heavy, and walk slowly towards the train.

I wonder if I should say goodbye? What makes me think that I am going to get away without a word being spoken? I hear a sharp intake of breath somewhere close behind me. God this is it. I hear the words before a single syllable is uttered. I must do something to stop it.

'How do you know?' The voice is harsh and accusing. I want to answer but dare not. 'What gives you the right to know what's best for me?'

I check myself. I must concentrate on keeping my voice under control. I must remain silent, present no argument whilst all aspects of my life are exposed by a screaming voice, shouting so loud people can hear it above the noisy confusion of the station. The same accusing questions are being mimicked by a delighted crowd and yelled into my face from all directions. 'What gives you the right to know what's best for me? How dare you assume that you have the power to read what's in my mind or feel the way I do? You who can't even begin to understand how much you mean to me?'

I can't explain my reasons, they are too complex for myself to fully understand. I must fight this urge to speak, to reply would be disastrous. My mouth is so dry my throat hurts. The accusations being directed at me come from a mouth twisted with fury, in a face distorted and ugly from sleeplessness and misunderstanding. Have I really reduced someone I care for to this state? Oh my God.

Those people have stopped loading their cases onto the train, interrupting their goodbyes to investigate the cause of this disturbance. Have they nothing to occupy their pathetic little minds? I suppose a bit of excitement will add spice to their dreary lives.

I hear you accuse me of not caring. It's simply not true. I can see that you are hurt, well so am I. I understand your anger but my so-called lack of experience is because I don't want to hurt you any more than I have done already.

That's why I stand here in silence, head bent, like a naughty school child listening to your voice, all your pent-up frustrations and abuse that fear has held back until now. I cringe at the things you are yelling at me. I hope that in the cold clear light you will realise that you didn't really mean them. I must steel myself not to shout back or give in, as I have done before. You are shouting again, the persuasive voice fades into a jumble of words. If only I could answer you, if only. I could explain to myself.

Hell that hurts. I can feel the pain caused by my nails digging into the soft flesh of my palms. If I apply more pressure perhaps the pain will help to blot out all the accusing hateful words which are, perhaps deservedly, being hurled at me. I know that most of them will be regretted. I realise that they are being used to inflict the pain of revenge. My heart is hurting, surely it can be heard. I will try to look beyond this outburst of temper, convinced that I am doing the right thing.

Just look at all those pathetic people blatantly listening. Look at them staring and nudging one another. Some of them are making no secret of the fact that they are enjoying listening to every embarrassing, revealing word. One or two are moving towards us making aggressive gestures. Oh no, not that too, not here. I don't know what to do, I don't think I can cope.

Now tinged with hysteria the abuse continues.

'What am I going to do without you, have you even considered that?' The question flies into the smoke-filled dome and echoes around my head. If I clamp my hands over my ears I might shut out the words.

'All aboard,' the voice of the over-zealous guard and the noise of carriage doors being slammed breaks the tension of the situation and allows my escape.

'Hurry, hurry,' the guard demands again.

At any other time I might find the incident amusing, listening to that man one might be forgiven for assuming that it is the passengers who are holding up the train and not the train being twenty minutes late.

I must get on this train. I can taste the salt of tears as I brush my lips gently against familiar sun-tanned cheeks. I must not allow our lips to touch or to look into those soft imploring eyes with their promise of such sensuous pleasure. I feel my groin tingle. I squeeze my eyelids tightly together to prevent the thoughts becoming a reality that I am too weak to resist. I remember how many times we have played this or other similar scenes before. This must be the last. Come on pull yourself together, pick up your bags and get on the train. It is becoming obvious that the majority of the passengers are not going to board the train until they have seen the incident through to its bitter end. I will just have to steel myself to walk through these people, both the sympathetic and the hostile and fight down the feeling of fear of both of them.

Suddenly I have had enough. I am tired of it all. I will just let things carry on as they were. I shudder with apprehension at the look in those sad eyes. I realise that there is no going back. Too much has been said. Now the argument is over. I wonder if you know how close you were to winning. Quick climb aboard the train and slam the door. My breathing is short and painful as though I have just run a mile in under four minutes. Take some deep breaths, try to regain some composure. Now the passengers quickly board the impatient train, I notice that they all make a point of avoiding my carriage. It's just as well I'm in no mood for company. Automatically I let the window down and stand silent and useless, my eyes averted from the window.

I can feel tears on my cheeks and the tightness in my throat is becoming unbearable. I feel a shudder, the train is moving. The feeling of relief is overwhelming but guilt berates me for feeling that way. A blast of noise and steam fills the air, for a moment it stuns me. Now I can hear the sound of iron wheels on iron tracks. Without thinking I thrust my hand through the still open window. It seems the only thing left for me to do. I am so afraid of the decision I have made, afraid of the loneliness that the future will bring. I am so unsure of everything, especially leaving. Someone has grabbed my hand, the pull on my arm is strong. I won't let go. I shall just hold on to this hand until it drags me from the train to die beneath its impatient iron wheels. The train is gathering speed. The hand is being gradually dragged from my grasp. The clinging fingers are finally pulled apart, my hand is left reaching out into emptiness.

'Goodbye,' I am shouting as loud as I can into the steam-filled air. I am sure that I can hear a reply, goodbye, the voice is faint, already fading away into the increasing space between us. I am so terrified, all I want to do is push the carriage door open, jump down on to the platform and return to the life I am so quickly leaving behind. I grasp the door handle, in my panic I am trying to push the door open, but the train is already moving too fast, the pressure of the wind pushes back, it's too late. I am sure that I can hear the words, 'Never forget me.' I never will, I never will. I'll stay here at the window and let the wind cool my face and ruffle my hair. I am beginning to feel a little calmer and thoughts, which have been repressed during the last few hours, clamour to be heard again.

The last few years have been good, very good, in fact the happiest time I shall ever know, but unfortunately we live in an imperfect world, things very rarely turn out the way we would have them. I have tried really hard but I knew, even in my happiness, that it could not last. That's why at times friends could not understand why I was sad. I knew from experience that I must not allow myself to become too committed or take the responsibility for someone else's happiness. I find it hard to take another's needs into consideration. I need to be free. Able to do as I want when I want. Someone sooner or later will find out that I haven't yet learned to cope with reality. I am selfish and weak, maybe, certainly not very brave. I haven't got the guts to face the world, to stand up and be counted for my beliefs. Perhaps in a few years when others have achieved a more understanding world I shall regret this decision that it is better that I leave now while all our memories, except our parting, are happy ones, before the recriminations begin. Before the feeling of being trapped and scared of being found out cause me to betray someone I love. Perhaps as I have reason to know, beyond help. I shall probably never share my life again. It wouldn't be fair. I am very much afraid of growing old and being alone. I must stop this morbid thinking, life will happen the way it dictates without consulting me, worry or not.

I am feeling cold leaning out of the window. Without wanting them certain memories are forcing everything else from my mind. I know I am going to cry. I cannot stop it. Here I am, standing, alone at the open window of a train steaming its way through the fresh green countryside of rural England. My tears turning into deep racking sobs running uncontrolled through my body. I can now allow myself to admit my faults and uncertainties, but only to myself. I feel guilt and compassion for the one I abandoned without adequate explanation. I weep selfishly for myself and the uncertainties and fears for my future, then almost with relief I cry unrestrained for the perverse ironies of life that make us what we are without giving us the abilities to understand why.

UNEVENTFUL

Susan Mullinger

Charlie Scott decided that she would move from the stretched position she had adopted on her three seat settee. She would move in another few minutes, after all what are a few minutes? Charlie had been lying down for several hours.

She was holding her television remote and thinking that she would go and make a cup of coffee. But settled on her pink draylon covered settee it seemed impossible for her to stand. Why rush? twenty-seven-year-old Charlie thought - I am not intending to go anywhere. Later, I could have a long relaxing soak in the bath and my hair could do with a wash, if I can just summon up some much needed energy. Charlie was aware it was almost a week since she had cleansed her short but naturally curly hair and it was looking greasy.

But still Charlie lay down and carried on flicking through the television channels, until she heard the continuity announcer state that a rerun of 'Coronation Street' was about to start. Charlie had loved watching this programme since she was a young girl. She settled down by pressing her head back against her pink and blue cushion. Charlie made sure her perfect size six body felt relaxed as the familiar signature tune began.

She decided during the half-time advert break, a call of nature wanted answering. Charlie dragged her body into an upright position and marched herself into the downstairs lavatory. On the way back to the lounge, she grabbed a newly washed blanket which had been left on a chair in the hallway. It was on top of a pile of washing waiting patiently to be taken upstairs.

That's better, much warmer, Charlie thought, as she quickly resumed her prone status. It was from here she enjoyed the rest of the programme. Now, she thought, it is time for coffee and perhaps something light to eat. There are only a few minutes before an old version of 'Countdown' is screened. Maybe I will prepare something after I have watched the programme and then have my meal tonight.

Throughout the programme Charlie shouted answers at the screen. 'It is quite exhausting,' she remarked out loud, trying hard to stifle a yawn. 'Countdown' finished and Charlie felt it was definitely time for a coffee. Hearing her stomach rumble she decided to get a snack. Finding the remains of a stale loaf Charlie scraped off the mould and applied a thick layer of blackcurrant jam to a thick wedge of bread. This was easier to do than make toast she surmised.

When Charlie carried her bread and mug of black coffee back to the lounge she was aware of her telephone ringing in the hall. She ignored the repeated ringing tone, believing that the unknown caller would ring back if there was an emergency. At the moment Charlie was in no rush to speak to anyone.

She did have a slight worry. For several hours Charlie knew there was something wrong and because of the problem she should be taking some sort of action. Unfortunately she seemed incapable of remembering the nature of the problem. Charlie put the matter to one side while she became involved in a panel game being shown on a Freeview channel. She adored quizzes, particularly enjoying general knowledge questions. It had always seemed to her that her brain retained the strangest of facts which she would use to amuse family and friends.

Once the panel game was over it was time for more caffeine with lots of sugar. Charlie did not take milk, in fact, she did not like pure dairy products but was a renowned chocoholic. It did not matter what kind but she consumed at least two bars of chocolate each day. Her friends were envious that she could eat so much without putting on an ounce of weight. Charlie put this ability down to her quick metabolism for which she was extremely grateful.

Oh bother! she thought, there goes the telephone again. It did not seem to be stopping, that was until Charlie stood up to answer it and the ringing ended. A loud bang heralded the arrival of the post. The letter box always made a clanging sound because of the strong spring mechanism. I expect, thought Charlie, there'll be at least two utility bills, they always come in pairs and a letter from my maiden aunt. The latter will be several pages long containing news of various funerals my aunt has attended in the last couple of weeks. It is Wednesday and therefore there will be lots of leaflets describing offers for which I have been specially chosen. I will leave the mail until later, Charlie decided. She thought, there is no point in upsetting myself and she reached for the biscuit barrel and was pleased to extract a plain digestive for dunking in her drink.

Charlie effortlessly drifted off to sleep and was surprised to find it was almost four o'clock when she awoke. Feeling peckish Charlie headed for her fridge freezer, which was positioned in a corner of her extremely small kitchen. It was narrow enough for Charlie to stand arms outstretched and be able to touch both sides. Inside the freezer Charlie was spoilt for choice. She removed a ready meal for one and placed it in the microwave. Once the meal of roast chicken and vegetables was cooked, Charlie took it to the table in the lounge to eat. She did not remove the plastic dish believing she was making less washing up, anything for an easy life.

Eating her meal Charlie glanced out of the bay window at the rain, which had continued unabated all day. Already daylight was fading and it was necessary to put on the standard lamp. This enabled Charlie to scan her copy of the Radio Times before again heading for the downstairs lavatory in her fluffy slippers. Her young niece called them her granny slippers but Charlie felt the cold and anything which made her feel comfortable was good. On her way to the little room she put the plastic dish in the bin in the kitchen.

The only noise she heard was the sound of an inherited heirloom which had been handed down several times. This was an elegant grandmother clock which chimed regularly on the hour. A magnificent example of workmanship but it did not fit in with furnishings in other rooms therefore, it lived in the hallway. The clock looked splendid like a soldier standing proudly on guard duty. Its mahogany case did not appear odd in the hall. Most of the other furniture was pine and characterless. The clock reminded Charlie of childhood and happy days.

Returning to the lounge and noting it was now five past five, Charlie still had a nagging doubt that there was something she should be doing other than making an effort to wash and dress. It was unusual to take a day off from work but Charlie knew her bosses owed her several holiday days. She thought, I do not suppose they have missed me and the office will not close down because of my absence. I wonder if it is too early to have a glass of wine, perhaps, it will give me some colour in my cheeks. 'I will only have a small one,' she said out loud, 'because I've got a thumping headache.' Charlie poured some full-bodied red wine and looked at her post. As she had predicted two bills, a long letter from her aunt and a leaflet describing the latest in modern hearing aids. Charlie poured another glass of wine, thinking, this is not bad for cheap supermarket plonk.

Time passed but finally Charlie decided it was time to go and freshen up. She washed her hair before having a shower. Naked, Charlie approached her bedroom door and was about to enter the room when she remembered what she had to do. Charlie ran downstairs and lifted the telephone receiver.

She dialled the number and the unseen operator said, 'Which emergency service do you require?'

In a calm voice Charlie replied, 'Police because I have killed my husband Steve Scott. I did it this morning, he's upstairs in bed.'

The operator asked Charlie if she was sure Steve was dead but she replied that she had shot him with his shotgun, when he fell asleep. He had not moved. Charlie continued, 'He will never be able to cheat on me with his secretary again, I smelt her perfume on him the last two nights when he was supposed to be working late.'

Avoiding the carnage in the bedroom Charlie dressed but almost fell over the gun which was lying at the end of the bed in her hurry to go and answer the doorbell. Many times Charlie had asked Steve if he and his secretary were having an affair but he always denied it. Rumours had reached her ears that he felt unable to resist Lydia's charms and Charlie felt humiliated. Thus when she opened her door to two policemen all she felt was relieved, after all it was a fait accompli.

FOR WHOM THAT BELL TOLLED!

Sara Swatt

A bell rang. I opened my eyes and thought, Oh no! Not him, anyone but him!

When and how did it come to this? We were so much in love at the start; never wanting to leave each other's side. Now, I shiver and tremble when he is in the house. What happened to us, in only five years of marriage?

It was a very warm, sunny August afternoon. Jenny and I were sipping our iced coffees, sitting outside in the shade of The Curious Café, 'our local'!

'Whoa! Which wonderful planet did he come from? I bet his name is Apollo!'

This was Jenny in her usual 'I don't chase boys, I just love them' voice as she tossed her rich, auburn shoulder-length hair, flashing her green eyes at the man approaching us from across the road.

'Hello! Irene, I hoped I would see you here. I remembered you said this café was a favourite haunt of yours. How are you?'

And this was Steve, senior prefect and captain of our school football team and soon to be attending medical school. He would need to be a doctor if he was going to have such an affect on the female species - if Jenny's outburst and reaction was anything to go on.

* * * *

Ten years later Steve and I were married; Jenny was my only bridesmaid. We had flown off to the Bahamas for a surprise tropical wedding. Two days after that Jenny returned home and we enjoyed the rest of the month for our honeymoon. It was paradise! My 'husband ... husband' what a lovely sound; I am his 'wife'. Two beautiful words to be savoured for eternity.

* * * *

Three years later I received a call from the hospital. There had been an accident when one of the patients in reception became violent. Steve came between the patient and the nurse attending. The patient grabbed one of the fire extinguishers off the floor, swung it up and somehow caught Steve's left hand and rammed it against the wall. He felt and heard the sound of bones being crushed and broken before he fell to the floor writhing in pain. His left hand was badly damaged. Then he felt as if his head had split open; the patient's boot had struck him on the temple. Steve passed out as security men got hold of the patient.

When he came to, he realised he was now a patient in a single side ward. His head was bandaged over one eye; his left hand was in soft-plaster up to the forearm but leaving the thumb and fingers free. He stayed in that ward for a month during which time he was being monitored, not only for the hand, but also with brain scans. He kept going in and out of fainting spells. Steve was in a serious state from the kick to the head.

His surgeon days were suddenly over. He was just 31 years of age and crippled (as he later began to refer to himself).

We were fortunate enough, through the hospital medical insurance, to have the full-time services of a nurse trained to take care of particular trauma cases. She was young but knew what she had to do - and was very patient with both of us. The hand was very slowly repairing; he could move his fingers a little. It was his head that was troubling him a lot; his eyesight was also affected by double vision just before he would black out. These would last from twenty to thirty minutes before he slowly came round again. But they left him with terrible migraines.

After eighteen months of careful nursing, more brain scans and physiotherapy for his hand, Steve seemed to feel much better and discharged the nurse.

Going back to work was ruled out by his medical team at the hospital. They could not risk Steve suddenly having double vision and a blackout, even though these were now few and far between. The stress of work might trigger these off without warning. Steve would now be a liability. He realised that they had to be firm; the 'compensation culture' loomed like a dark cloud. This made hospitals and practitioners wary - almost to the point of stress. This could only impede their concentration in case anything did not work out to the patient's needs and satisfaction. Steve realised he was no use to the profession in his present medical state.

The following three years changed him so much. I just didn't know what to do, or how to act to make his life, and mine, more comfortable. Against his wishes, I arranged with the hospital, and our own doctor, for a nurse with physiotherapy experience to call in twice a week to see Steve. She needed to stay only a couple of hours each day then I would take over, having by now learned what I should do for him.

Where had my Steve, my beautiful husband, gone? In such a short while, life had dealt both of us a cruel blow - but especially for Steve. Everything I did or tried to do for him was useless, he would shout at me. Then he began to use abusive language; I ignored this at first and put it down to frustration at his physical problems. Because of his physical state, we had been sleeping in separate bedrooms. I felt so helpless; what could I do to make Steve's life easier? Nothing could compensate for his loss.

* * * *

Steve and I separated. He moved into a bachelor flat and I stayed in the house. I was now working full-time as a practice nurse in a general practitioners' clinic near home. He used to call in occasionally but seemed to be moving around dazed. At first I felt so sorry for him, but lately his changes of mood were getting from bad to worse. I dreaded his visits and told him it would be better for both of us if he stayed away. Divorce proceedings had started and, under the circumstances, I was happy for the arrangements offered by the solicitors. I just could not take any more of Steve's visits. I became stressful and fearful.

One evening, after I had said goodbye to some close friends I had invited to dinner, I had just prepared for bed when I heard the doorbell ring. One of my friends must have left something behind. But something about the way the bell was buzzing, a cold dread caught hold of me. I slipped into my house-coat slowly. I went down the stairs and up to the front door. I looked through the peep-hole and froze. What was he doing here at this late hour? I became icy cold with fear. The bell rang again with an insistence that would brook no denial and I thought, Oh no! Not him, anyone but him. It was obvious that he would not go away until I opened the door to him. By now the neighbours would have heard the continuous buzzing of the bell. I took a deep breath, braced myself and opened the door.

He stood there looking quite wretched. I could not help but feel pity for him. The pity that comes from remembered love and not with contempt. I let him in quietly and closed the door. As I turned round to face him, he walked gently towards me and put his arms around me. Surprised at his action, but feeling the gentle way in which he held me, I looked up and met his eyes, 'Can we talk a while; I have missed you.'

I led him into the sitting room and offered him a soft drink. He declined. He seemed to be struggling with his thoughts. He then put his face in his hands and bowed his head. I had never known Steve to be lost for words. He was always confident and cheerful, that is, before the awful things that had happened to him. Then he changed and had become violent, but still, never lost for words.

'What is it?' I asked quietly.

'I am so sorry for the things I have put you through since I lost my profession. I was wrong to take it out on you. You were always very supportive, loving and loyal. What have I done to us - we had something so special. How did I spoil it?' His voice came in a thick, slow, soft sound.

In that moment my heart went out to him. I reached out my hand and took his injured left hand in mine.

'Circumstances were building up seemingly against us, almost to deliberately destroy what we had. Perhaps we should have known that our special relationship would have its trials. We were just not prepared; we were too happy. Neither of us was to fault. It just happened.'

'Do you think there is any possibility that we may put the past behind us and start again? Or is that too much to expect after all I have made you endure.'

All I could say was, 'We could but try, taking it one step at a time and not expecting too much from each other immediately. A sort of wooing each other in the old-fashioned way.'

He looked up and gave me one of his old Steve smiles.

'How quaintly you have put it. But, if you agree, I would like a second chance. We had a few good years at the start. Perhaps we can try and remember how happy we were then. That might help us.'

He stood up and pulled me gently out of the armchair. 'May I stay the night with you. I would be happy to use one of the smaller rooms, if you prefer it.'

Suddenly I woke up! Doubt entered my mind. Was he being genuinely remorseful, or was I being too soft in the head? I looked up at him but could see no guile in his eyes.

'Come and help me prepare the spare bedroom at the front of the house.'

I led the way upstairs, with him following slowly behind. As we approached the landing he quickened his pace and caught me around the waist. I looked back at him smiling. Then I froze. His grip round my waist tightened, vice-like. I shouted at him to stop as he was hurting me. I found myself being pressed up against the banister. Then with one mighty swoop he lifted me off the floor. I screamed in panic but this only seemed to urge him on. He lifted me up onto the rail, grabbed me by my left hand and swung me over. I struggled to no avail.

Then he let go of my hand and I fell and kept falling …

THE GYPSY AND THE VICAR

Peter Jennison

She was a natural beauty, tall and tanned, with jet-black hair which hung in waves about her shoulders. For a daughter of the travellers born to a life in the open air she was remarkably soft and elegant. She had hazel eyes, that look of pure innocence, and a smile to melt the hardest of hearts. But she knew the world and from the age of fourteen had worked things out and found her place in it. As the years went by she grew more desirable and now, at the age of twenty-two, was a beautiful voluptuous young woman.

She lived in a camper van and read the ladies' palms at local fairs. All men wanted her, only one caught her fancy from time to time, and only then because his shy denial touched on her whimsical spirit. His name was Hadrian, vicar of the neighbourhood parish. She would see him at shows and other outdoor gatherings she attended. He was a man of some standing was this young vicar, which appealed to her, cultured, respected, trusted. But a man after all and his connection with the church made her musing all the more thrilling. She would drive to his village at the end of each day and park overnight near the vicarage.

To the vicar her arrival was that of a stranger to his flock, so he visited her each month as he did other souls who lived alone in the parish. She welcomed his visits, spicing the hour with smiles and lingering glances. He would be hard to win, but was young and fit and, according to gossip, struggling with his vow of celibacy. Of course there was a love in his life already - God - but this only added that extra thrill to her adventure. She mused to herself as she thought of him. She would have him - she would - and she knew she would. Men were such fools against the blazing flame of femininity.

And she was halfway there if she did but know because the vicar, a boy in experience but in years a man nearing thirty, had himself forbidden feelings for the sultry dark-eyed beauty. He fought against them certainly, truly he did, but was losing ground with every visit. In the month of May he called round one evening and found her in a flimsy silk negligee. The game was on, and the soothsayer's prediction about to be made a reality.

'Come in,' she said. 'No need for ceremony in this van.'

So this was the vicar's big moment. He stayed until dawn then saw in the first hour of daylight. He was torn naturally, ashamed on the one hand but thrilled to be with her on the other. He analysed his feelings and believed their intimacy a true expression of love. This was love, the eternal, the reality of which was her still in his arms and him wanting her! He held her close, felt her flesh against his and marvelled. He was a new man, touched by the spirit and born into real love at last.

'I am gone,' he uttered softly looking in her eyes, 'melted away, gone in your limbs and flesh.'

She only laughed at him.

So the naïve vicar felt love and tenderness towards her. He began to consider them biblically. She was Eve and he Adam whom the Lord had blessed, and who together in one love on this silvery dawn were the first born spirits risen from the dust of Creation. His heart swelled and love felt enormous as he thought this. He watched her in stillness, her eyes, her lips, the cute little wrinkles which gathered about her nose when she laughed. And she was everything.

'I must get up,' he said at last, hauling himself slowly from under her.

She let him escape but only to watch and savour the thrill of her success.

'You are a beautiful man,' she said.

Then she kissed him at the door and off he went light as feathers.

As he drove, he considered his situation. He had never known such a night. He was floating on air and the world was floating along with him. It was the first dawn of the first day, with the world in wonder at the newborn pulse of creation. The morning dew had covered the hedgerows with diamonds, and the rising sun was ascending on angels' wings. He would marry the woman, have her at the vicarage and redeem himself. And why not - she loved him.

In her absence he watched and waited like a dog for her camper van. His sermon on the Sunday was passionate and forgiving, full of tenderness. From Primrose Hill he could see above the roofs and out to her space between the beech trees, and at every opportunity climbed the steep bank to look for her. When at last she appeared his heart skipped as if to be the death of him. He put on a suit and walked the half mile to meet her. She was everything by now, the blood in his veins, the light in his soul, the very breath in him. A more genuine love had never been found or even dreamt of. He tapped lightly on her door.

'Oh Hadrian,' she said, 'how lovely. Do come in.'

He sat in the window and she went briefly to her bedroom. He watched her draw the curtain and disappear. When she opened it again and stood with the rosy glow behind her she took his breath away. He prepared to go down on one knee.

'Cindy,' he began. 'Would you do me ...'

'Of course,' she put in, 'anything for you, only this time all night is forty pounds.'

THE COMPANY OF PROPHETS

Bill Hayles

The weekend at the mountain refuge seemed to last forever, but as the sun rose majestically into the crisp Welsh air the trumpets sounded calling the tripartite army of God to assembly. On a raised platform backed by huge plasma screens the three patriarchs addressed the brotherhood.

'Brothers and sisters, on Friday the storm clouds of war gathered above us and the enemy overwhelmed us with their sudden assault. We were caught on the wrong foot and retreated in disarray, shocked and confused. But this is a new day and the flood waters have been repulsed. Our friendly politicians, church leaders, lawyers and law officers have set in motion a chain of events that have the enemy reeling. The downside is that the attack of the financial institutions owned by the bonesmen has caused the collapse of financial services worldwide, we may be heading into a global credit crunch. There will follow fifteen years of financial famine and drought and we must guide our people through it safely, the work ahead is mammoth. The four existing 'Lances of Christ' which are in fact the spears of the four horsemen of the apocalypse held in the four holy places around the world have become active, so the Eschatological days grow ever nearer, the final battle is afoot. Return now to your Citadels and prepare for war! Evangelise your communities, politicise your neighbours and bring down the neo-con governments and their minions. Cast out those who cause schism between our three churches, the time has come for the three children of God to stop their sibling rivalry and to stand as one against the enemy. Let our watch words be 'One Father God - three mother churches.' Now go, and God go with you all.'

The people began to disperse and Appleforth caught up with Nat and Michael and said, 'Well this is it brothers, we are going home, and Muhammad Iqbal and the Islamic group, and David Ben Harim and his Hebrew group are coming with us, the Citadel will be the main co-ordination centre for the Tripartite covenant!'

Nat smiled and said, 'That will be good, the dome has always felt empty, and we will need to increase our farm and stock sizes.'

Michael added, 'And the accommodation pods, we will have to open up the dome's visitor centre and lecture blocks.'

Appleforth nodded and said, 'But we will have many more hands to make the work light, let's get our people rounded up and on the road, I can't wait to get back home.'

By lunch the Citadel convoy was preparing to descend the Welsh mountain roads and head south once more when the cavern was shaken by a great explosion. The main doors exploded inwards showering tons of debris everywhere. Some of the pieces weighed over a ton in weight, and several vehicles parked by the doors were flattened: thank the Lord, all were empty or the death toll would have been in the hundreds. The cavern lights all went out as one plunging the refuge into a dark and dusty night. Nat stiffened and turned slowly to face the now open entrance and he cried out, 'Demons … to arms … to arms!'

Other prophets around the great hall were taking up the cry and the priests were forming prayer circles and calling down the Angelic host. Vile flying horrors swooped down from the blackness firing their flaming poisonous arrows indiscriminately but worse things were abroad on the cavern floors. Vile creatures, the distorted creations of Satan poured in through the breach and the community were forming small islands of fighting men and women with the children in the centre of the circles. Through the eye-stinging dust Nat saw what at first appeared to be a dinosaur lurching towards him, but as fires, which were springing up everywhere, illuminated the huge beast he saw it was in fact a Wyvern. A Wyvern is smaller than a dragon, and has only two legs, not four. Its bat-like wings had tiny claws at the outer tip but they were of no danger; not so its breath which spewed forth deadly plague, and its tail carried a nasty sting which was also painfully deadly. Nat closed his eyes and raising his hands towards Heaven he cried, 'Lord send Elijah's fire from Heaven ... smite this beast of Hell.'

He could feel the breath of the beast, it was that close and its smell was overpowering and made him want to heave, but a small yellow ball appeared near the ceiling and grew bigger and bigger until a huge yellow ball of fire struck the Wyvern worm and consumed it claw and scale. Nat fell to his knees exhausted, but he muttered a prayer of thanks under his breath. Looking up he saw a huge aboriginal man slowly running towards him brandishing a huge wooden club, it was a Nephilim, one of the giants mentioned in Exodus who lived before and after the great flood. Nat closed his eyes and said, 'O Lord the God of Abraham, Isaac and Jacob, give me the strength of Samson.'

The Nephilim swung the huge bough towards Nat's head but he ducked under it and grabbed the giant by his chain link belt, he hoisted him off his feet and threw him with a crash into the nearby wall, knocking him senseless.

Nat stared at the carnage of battle all around him, there were exploding demons everywhere. A pack of satanic dogs were running in fear from the fires that raged everywhere and trying desperately to find the way out. Flashes of silver lightning lit the cavern as the newly arrived Angelic host fired bolt after bolt at the creatures writhing below. The islands of defenders had begun to link up with neighbours, and the children had been led to safety in a side canyon that could be easily defended by a few prophets and a prayer circle. Nat could feel his strength returning and he knew that the other prophets were getting the same image in their heads as he was. He was seeing a circle of blue-white light as bright as the sun hovering in his mind like a mighty halo. The light became an arc above his head and the other prophets positioned themselves around the cavern walls and the glowing arks began to link together until the whole cavern was encompassed by the ring of light. The prophets slowly raised their hands and the ring rose into the air. Every demon the ring passed exploded into red dust, and on the ground, at the same instant, a creature controlled by that exploding demon ceased to be. As the halo reached the roof, there were only real animals and evil men left below. Finding themselves alone and surrounded by fighting men and angels they panicked, the packs of dogs and other living beasts turned on the evil men who were thrown into disarray and who began fighting each other to get away from the animals and angels until all lay dead on the ground.

The defenders stood panting and sweating, glad to have survived the carnage, but then sorrow followed when they began to pick out the bodies of fallen saints among the dead. Healers were moving among the corpses looking for any who might be saved, many were, they were lifted gently and carried to hospital tents that had sprung up away from the battleground, but when the counting was done, three hundred and forty-six saints had died and two hundred and fifty had sustained injuries needing attention. The fallen were buried outside the refuge on the gentle slopes of the mountain facing eastward so that they would greet the return of the Lord. After a service for the dead and the injured the groups began to leave and head for their own Citadels, and Nat sat beside Appleforth who wore a bandage around his forehead and his right arm was in a sling and he said, 'Do you think that was the last ditch battle of a defeated foe, or are there such days ahead?'

Appleforth shook his head softly from side to side and said with a sigh in his voice, 'I fear that the enemy is far from defeated Nat, we have wounded him deeply that is for sure, but like the seven-headed dragon in the Book of Revelation, we have severed one head with a mortal blow, but the beast lives and has six more heads.'

Nat checked his mirrors as he pulled around a sheep grazing in the road. 'I noticed in the fight I was able to call on the powers of biblical prophets and judges to defeat the enemy. Am I going to retain those powers?'

Appleforth smiled and said, 'Not retain the powers as such, but as your spirit grows stronger, you will be able to access any of God's gifts that you need for any purpose, be it fire from Heaven, parting waters with your cloak, bringing food and water from the heavens, even bringing forth water from the desert. You can use the strength of Samson, the wisdom of Solomon or the fighting skills of David and Joshua. You are the twenty-first century prophet, the end times are near, and Armageddon draws ever closer.'

Nat sat in silence for a while concentrating on his driving but at last he asked, 'Why couldn't we raise our fallen brothers after the battle? This is one of God's gifts!'

Appleforth replied, 'Everybody has a time to be born and a time to die, this battle was written in the book of life, and they have gone to be with the Lord. They are not abandoned, but exalted. We will lose many more brave saints before this war is over, all we can hope to do is God's will, and to serve him to the utmost of our ability. We will never forget our fallen brothers and sisters, but we will be reunited with them after the final battle, and the celebration will last for eternity.'

They reached the Citadel before dark, and were surprised to find the damage done by the police and social services on the night of the flight from danger had been repaired, and the members of local churches had been running the farm and making ready for their return. The Tripartite union still did not fill the dome, and Appleforth advised the church leaders to bring their people into the protection of the dome. But they declined, wishing to be out among the people, winning as many hearts and minds as they could before the end game. All Citadels were put on a war footing, and travel between each was only by well armed convoy and Angelic cover. In comparison the rest of the world went about its business as usual, fighting wars, losing and making money in the global recession and going about their daily lives oblivious to the spiritual welfare all around them. But that suited the Company of Prophets.

Nat and his kinsmen in the Citadel went about their daily chores too, farming and preaching, evangelising and teaching, and opening their doors at Easter and Christmas celebrating and selling crafts and singing songs. But while the local people slept safe at night tucked up in their beds, the Company of Prophets kept their lonely vigil watching over the gates of the abyss ready for any further breakout, prepared to put their lives on the line for those who mock and don't believe, those who believe science has all the answers, and even those who in their ignorance persecute the saints. The Tripartite army, one Father God … three mother churches … Jew, Muslim and Christian, half brothers and equal heirs to their Father's bounty, united at last against the one true enemy … Satan! God's got an army, it's not afraid to fight!

DANCING WITH ANGELS

Guy Fletcher

I haven't set foot in this small town for so many years. It seemed larger then and not so grubby. I have all but lost my Black Country accent and now find it rather comical: too much time living in London has obviously made me a bit of a snob! Today I am a wealthy man but I've nothing really to be proud of. I've been married twice, at this moment I'm alone again. Work saves me from the abyss of depression, although each dawn I die a little with remorse.

My best friend at school, Jack, has perished from cancer. He was captain of the rugby team but ended his life a pathetic, skeletal figure. Health, mental and physical, and love are the only ingredients which really matter in life. I would trade all my wealth for a contented mind, but alas, peace will not come.

I am sitting in the pub I used to frequent as a young man. There are some rough characters here who look at me with hostility, as if I'm a stranger, yet I visited here when they were in nappies. This pub too seems more rundown than in the past, or maybe that's my imagination. The window returns a ghost reflection of a man with an expensive suit but whose dreams have not been realised.

'So you returned then? Don't think that I've forgiven you. That I'll never do.'

'Jane. I can never forgive myself either. How is Emma?'

'Married. Three kids. Owns her own dance academy so pretty well really, except for the limp of course. You certainly left your mark boy. I don't think I'll linger if you don't mind.'

Thoughts from that horrific day infect my soul again. It is like an old film playing time and time again which I cannot delete. We had been drinking on that balmy summer evening when the sky was an Arabian blue and the future seemed just as glorious as the weather. Youth always thinks it's immortal, tragedy happens to others. I was laughing when it happened, travelling through the verdant country lane at a reckless speed. I was trapped. The second it took to realise my fate seemed to last for a century, feeling as doomed as if standing in front of a firing squad, just waiting for the impact. I remember briefly hearing Emma scream, a shattering, sickening sound and then oblivion.

At first I was treated with sympathy by the medics but when my alcohol levels proved positive then, oh, how the tide changed. I felt as though I was 'the villain of the Earth' as Enobarbus says to Antony. You see I'm a cultured fellow yet an idiot all the same. I escaped with only a few injuries but my psychological scars run far deeper.

Emma had the potential to become one of the greatest dancers this country has ever produced but in one moment her dreams were literally shattered. How cruel fate is: one never knows when disaster will strike. I often feel contempt for miserable Monday morning commuters with faces as glum as storm clouds, yet who possess their health and sanity.

Emma's dancing was majestic, it was dancing with angels. She had broken both of her legs and I was responsible. Our relationship shattered too and I was cast adrift like a lifeboat from a sinking ship. Work was my saviour but coming back here has re-opened old wounds, especially experiencing her sister's unforgiving demeanour. What did I expect, flowers and kisses? I was a drink-driver who had murdered her sister's dreams.

The Stella was sinking down extremely well this evening. I write Emma on the condensation of the cold pint as I watch her sister leave, throwing me a last withering glance which makes me wince as if I've been kicked in the shin. Finally I venture outside into the cold air, pulling up my collar. My breath is like ectoplasm as I walk unsteadily under a less then salubrious bridge with beer cans and cigarette butts strewn around like bodies on a battlefield and graffiti from some awful cro-magnon gang adorning the Victorian walls of the vile, urine-smelling place.

'You're the weirdo talking to himself in the pub, ain't you?'

'Look, I don't want any trouble, OK?'

'Oh, you've got trouble mate. Get him lads.'

My word, these youths are ugly: pizza faces and piggy eyes, dressed like some LA gangsters yet with a Bilston accent. I am trapped, just as I was in the car so many years ago and yet part of me longs to be hurt. They say self-harming relieves tension, I've never followed that road but I can see where they're coming from. I casually wonder if my body will end up in the foul canal.

'Jane said you were in town. My God, you're a mess.'

Am I dreaming? For I see Emma standing over me. Appearing elegant and yet with a walking stick. Age has treated her well. She seems serene whilst my youthful looks have disappeared and I'm certainly not at my best at this moment in time. I wipe blood from my mouth and know that tomorrow my body will ache from head to toe.

'I'm so sorry Emma. I guess I deserve a thousand beatings for what I've done to you.'

There is a man by her side, her husband I presume. A sudden surge of jealousy poisons my mind and then disappears like a snowflake on a river. I have never loved anyone like Emma and when I make love I close my eyes and think only of her.

'That was a long time ago. I hated you for a while but living a life full of hatred is no life. I pulled myself together, as they say - the past is a foreign country. I forgive you. Now let us get you cleaned up.'

Am I dreaming? I feel myself drifting back into unconsciousness but maybe I'm already there.

THE MIDNIGHT VISITOR

Audrey Allen

It had been a long dark day; low black clouds hung over the old house in an almost macabre manner. Then, at six o'clock, the heavens opened, the rain came down as if to drown the whole Earth, the wind was so strong that the great old oak trees were bending from side to side as if being moved by a giant hand. Never in her life had Mary seen such a terrible storm; she was very afraid; she was alone in the house. The house that had been in the family for generations; she loved the old house, she had missed it so much when she married John and they had had to move away to London to be near John's office, a law firm started by his father many years before. They were very happy in the flat that John's father had given them for a wedding present but Mary had still missed her childhood home set in its own grounds, surrounded by a beautiful wood. Then, one glorious day for Mary, John's father decided to open a new office out of London and to Mary's joy it was in the village of Twinway, very close to her old home where, at the time, her mother still lived with Nancy, her companion of many years. The good news was that John was to run this branch. Mary's mother, who was very excited that her daughter was returning to the area, offered them a home with her; it was a large house so they could live their separate lives; John was happy to agree. Everything was wonderful, they were all so very happy.

That was ten years ago. For nine years everything was perfect, but just a year ago Mary's mother had died and Nancy moved back with her family, so whenever John had business in London, Mary was on her own, which normally did not worry her. But today - there were no words to describe how she felt - there was something wrong, she could feel it in the air, but must pull herself together, she must be brave, she had supper to prepare and she must open the door and let Marcus the cat in. It was no use waiting any longer for her husband to return from London; she had just heard on the radio that the bridge that linked them with the village had been washed away. She was alone!

What was happening? The house was shaking as if in the middle of an earthquake, the thunder and lightning was so violent it was lighting the whole house, the wind rose even higher, it was so unreal. Mary moved slowly along the wall, she must reach the window to see what was happening. She stared out into the night and jumped as a flash of lightning struck the window, at the same time lighting the edge of the woods where, to Mary's horror, she could see a figure dressed all in black moving towards the house. She could not see its face - it was like something from a horror film.

Mary stood rooted to the spot trembling all over. She must pull herself together - there was no one there. Who would be out there on a night like this? She laughed to herself, it was all in her imagination. What was that sound? Footsteps on the gravel drive! Something or someone was moving towards the house, slowly, quietly, getting nearer with every step. A piercing scream from the nearby woods, as a cat, owl or some other creature stalked its prey, made it pause for a brief moment. Then on it came, nearer and nearer until it almost reached the large old house. Then, as if by magic, the storm ceased. The dark clouds which had caused so much rain in such a short space of time, broke, to allow a full moon to light the heavy oak door. As Mary stood looking at the door, she froze to the spot as she could hear, on the other side of the door, a key being placed in the lock - it was turning slowly. Mary waited, horrified, in the darkness of the hall. She moved behind the darkly stained staircase. She had heard no car and she knew from the radio report that John would not be home tonight - she was alone! She stifled a scream as the door swung open and the hand of a shadowy figure reached for the light switch. The next moment the hall was bathed in light and John stood looking at Mary who cried with relief. 'John! I didn't expect you, how did you get across the river? They said that the bridge was down.'

'Oh Mary, I'm so sorry I frightened you, I only wanted to surprise you, to be with you before midnight. I had to be with you for our twenty-fifth wedding anniversary, so I left the car on the other side and came across the old footbridge.'

'Oh John, that's wonderful! I thought we were going to have to celebrate it tomorrow. Come by the fire, you look so tired and you're very wet. I will get a dry towel and some hot soup, then we will open that champagne we have been saving, it's not quite midnight yet. John, while I get supper will you called Marcus in? The poor cat went out earlier and I called him for some time, then as it got late I was afraid to open the door.'

'That's not like you Mary.'

'I know John, I can't explain it.'

'Never mind Mary, I'll get Marcus in then we can open the champagne and you can open your present.'

John went to find Marcus and Mary went to the kitchen to make supper. Later as they sat down by the log fire, Mary served hot soup and newly made rolls. As John opened the champagne, Mary, with her hands shaking with excitement, undid the silver ribbon on her present and as the paper dropped away she found to her delight a bottle of the perfume she had worn on her wedding day.

'John! Where did you manage to find it? I haven't seen it in the shops for years.'

John smiled. 'Ah ... let's drink a toast then you can sit there by the fire. Marcus has already had his supper.'

They drank their toast and sat for a long time talking about their wedding day and all the people who had been with them, family, friends, the lovely little bridesmaids who were now grown up, married themselves and of course Mary's wonderful wedding dress which still hung in the attic. Tomorrow she would bring it down for a good sponge and press, she might even try it on. John laughed, 'Will it still fit?' He ducked as Mary threw a cushion at him which just missed Marcus - he was not very happy. John picked up the cushion and put it behind Mary's head. 'Close your eyes and relax,' so Mary closed her eyes, she did feel tired and the warmth of the fire lulled her to sleep. How long she slept for she did not know but she woke with a start as she heard the chime of the old grandfather clock from the hall. What time was it? The light was coming through the chinks in the curtains, the fire was out and old Marcus was sat looking at her, waiting for his breakfast. She sat counting the strokes of the clock - it was nine o'clock, how could that be and why had she slept in the chair and where was John? She smiled; he was probably in the kitchen preparing breakfast, dear John, always so kind and considerate but there was no sound from the kitchen and why was Marcus sat looking at her waiting for his breakfast?

Before she could get up from her chair, the telephone on the table beside her rang; Mary frowned, who was ringing her so early on a Sunday morning? She picked up the phone, 'Hello? Brackendale 415.'

It was Robert, John's oldest friend, he had also been best man at their wedding. He was then a young student doctor and had moved back into the village several years ago where he was doctor in charge of the cottage hospital. Before Robert could speak, Mary said, 'Don't tell me you and Sally can't join us for dinner tonight; John and I were looking forward to celebrating our twenty-fifth with you both.'

'Mary, Mary, please listen, I have been trying all night to reach you but before I tell you, you must understand all is well now.'

'Robert, what are you talking about?'

'Mary, please listen.'

'But Robert ... !'

'Mary, please listen! You must understand that all is well now.'

'Robert! What are you talking about?'

'Last night John had a very bad car accident.'

'But Robert ...'

'He was trying to get home to you.'

'But Robert, he did ...'

'Mary, please listen! I have to tell you, John was trying to get home to you for your anniversary but he had an accident when his car hit the old bridge - just before it was swept into the river. He was trapped in it as it turned over but luckily for him there was a car quite close behind. The occupants were strangers to the area and were following John's tail-lights hoping that he was leading them back to the main road. When the crash occurred, they acted very quickly and pulled John from his wrecked car in a matter of minutes. It was a miracle! They got John into their car, covered him well with blankets and realised that they must get him to a hospital as soon as possible, so they turned the car around and made it back to the crossroads and a signpost pointing to the hospital. When I first saw John he was quite out of his mind, saying that he must get home to you for your anniversary - then he went into a coma. At about ten minutes to midnight his heart stopped and I thought we had lost him - but Mary, he is going to be alright! Mary, are you still there? He's asking for you; if you can get to the old footbridge, I'll have a car waiting for you on the other side. Mary, do you understand?'

'Yes. Robert, I'm alright thank you. I'll start right away - tell John I love him and I'm coming. Goodbye Robert and thank you.'

As Mary put the phone down, she shivered - what had happened, had she been dreaming? And if it was a dream it was so vivid that she would never forget her nightmare that was so clear in her mind. Then she turned to see Marcus staring up at her - if she had been dreaming how did Marcus get in? But Marcus couldn't tell her ... Then as she went to stand up, her hand slipped down the side of the chair; she went cold with fear - her hand had rested on a small package. It was the bottle of her favourite perfume, no longer on sale in any shop, that had been brought to her by her midnight visitor.

SUSHI CAKE

Gina Dickerson

'I hate you!' screamed Nicole, her amber eyes blazing with fury.

The man on the bed hurriedly forced his legs into his jeans, stumbling in his haste. 'You're overreacting,' he complained.

Nicole curled her top lip in disdain. 'Overreacting?' she echoed. 'Actually Darren, I think I'm being quite calm.'

Darren's tanned, muscular arms reached for her. 'I'm sorry babe.'

Nicole shook her head. 'Sorry that you've got caught?'

She took in the sight of the bed, the pink satin sheets rumpled, the taffeta duvet pushed to the bottom. The blonde hair, fanned across a pillow, the owner unmoving. She shuddered at the screwed up, obviously used tissues, strewn on the floorboards. Then she saw them. The pink, furry handcuffs tossed to the end of the bed. She reached for them and something inside her snapped.

'Callie!' she hollered, throwing the cuffs towards the figure at the head of the bed. 'You bought me these on my hen night!'

Callie yelped as the cuffs hit her and sprung from the bed, she stood trembling in her nakedness. 'It was an accident.' She hung her head, her eyes pleading from beneath spiky lashes. With shaking hands she reached for her dress and slipped it on.

'Sure,' scoffed Nicole, raking a hand through her raven hair. 'He was laying there, with it ... it just sticking up and you happened to impale yourself on him while being completely naked, in my house, and then you found time to rummage in my wardrobe for the handcuffs, which, I know full well were in the box at the bottom of my wardrobe ... under all my jeans. It was no accident.' She felt tears brimming and silently willed herself not to burst out crying.

'I'll leave,' said Callie, edging past Nicole, unable to meet her gaze.

Nicole remained still, her back stiff. 'I don't want to see you again,' she said, without turning.

'But we've been friends for years,' stammered Callie. 'You've always been there for me, since we were at playschool together and you hit Robert Oliver for looking up my skirt.'

'I should've realised then what a tart you really are.'

Callie looked at her friend's back, her mouth silently opening and closing. She felt an overwhelming urge to reach out and wrap her arms around Nicole's rigid shoulders, but knowing that she had been instrumental in the tension she could not. Resignedly, she turned from the bedroom and slipped away.

Nicole pushed past Darren and furiously began tearing the bedding from her bed. 'This will have to be thrown away, I could never use any of this again knowing what has happened.' To her annoyance she felt the hot wetness of tears falling down her cheeks, trying to ignore them she continued removing the sheet, large drops plopping onto the satin and expanding upon contact.

'Don't cry,' implored Darren, his bare arms wrapping around her from behind. 'You don't need to.'

'I bloody well do,' sniffed Nicole. She twisted in his embrace until she was facing him. She looked at his blonde hair, fashionably cut, his blue eyes, clear and shining, his defined jaw, faintly shadowed by stubble and his straight, romanesque nose. She breathed in the familiar scent of his aftershave and kissed him softly on the lips. 'Get lost,' she murmured.

Darren took on a confused expression.

'You heard me,' said Nicole, her voice stronger this time. 'I don't want anything to do with you.'

'But we're engaged, we're getting married in two weeks.'

Nicole shrugged. 'You should've thought about that before you jumped into bed with her.' She stalked down to the kitchen, Darren chasing at her heels. 'I want you gone by the time I come back out,' she ordered.

With restraint, Nicole closed the kitchen door and poured herself a measure of cognac. Her hand was steady as she rose the glass to her lips and sipped, not even shuddering when the heat from the drink hit the back of her throat. She finished one glass and poured herself another while listening to the muffled sounds of her now ex-fiancé packing his belongings. She poured a third when he hesitantly pushed open the kitchen door and attempted to reason with her. She began a fourth when he gave up and left the house, slamming the front door behind him. She lost count of how many measures followed, she felt numb and alone.

Nicole was woken the following morning by the shaft of sunlight streaming across her face. Groggily she opened her eyes and groaned at the hardness of her pillow, stretching she realised that the pillow was so hard because it was not actually a pillow. It was the cold, kitchen floor. Her tongue was stuck to the roof of her mouth and she ached, all over. Padding upstairs she forced herself to shower and stood under the pulsating fall, rivulets of water cascading down her tender body.

Nicole dressed mechanically and pulled her wedding organiser from her handbag. Feeling the worst she had in a long time, she set about the arduous task of telephoning to cancel arrangements.

Four hours, three boxes of tissues and one roll of toilet paper later, almost everything had been cancelled; she'd had to leave a message for the cake artist with a suspiciously dumb sounding man, who she doubted would remember anything she'd said. Although she was several hundred pounds lighter, Nicole still felt numb, it was as if she was watching the situation from the outside. She jumped as her mobile telephone began vibrating across the table. Nicole grabbed the phone before it fell and glared at the caller display. Darren. Tossing it beside her on the sofa, she decided to leave it to the answer-phone. Darren, she thought, could sod off. The phone rang for a second time and sighing in frustration, Nicole reached for it. Darren, again.

For the next ten minutes he called another twenty-five times and left three messages, each as pleading as the last. In which time, Nicole deftly applied a layer of make-up and unearthed her newest little black dress, one she had planned on wearing for the pre-wedding party because it accentuated her curves and made her already colt-like legs appear unfeasibly long. She tore the tags from it, not even wincing as the plastic bit into her finger. She ran a comb through her hair and slicked on a coat of enhancing lipgloss. Lovingly she reached to the top shelf of her wardrobe for the expensive gold, crystal encrusted sandals she had bought for her wedding day. Their straps curled exquisitely across her feet and up her ankles, they shimmered and glinted in the light, they made her feel sexy and desirable. Lucky, she thought dryly, considering that they had cost five hundred and thirty pounds. Her tan handbag looked incongruous with her outfit and she abandoned it, choosing to take her purse and mobile phone with her as she left the house.

Nicole teetered, really the sandals were extremely high and the heel impracticably thin, to the restaurant across the road. It was a modernistic, chic establishment that served sushi and fantastic cocktails. Nicole hated sushi, with a passion.

'Good evening madam,' drawled the bartender, a cute twenty-something in a tight fitting black top. 'What would you like?'

'You can start,' instructed Nicole, resting on a leather stool, 'by not calling me madam. I'm neither married nor old.'

The bartender grinned, displaying perfect white teeth so that Nicole was momentarily jealous. 'What shall I call you then?'

'Nicole,' replied Nicole, a hint of a smile playing on her lips.

'Andy.' The younger man returned her smile. 'I can recommend Sex With The Waiter.'

'What?' Nicole laughed. 'We've only just met, besides I'm probably ten years older than you.'

'No,' said the bartender patiently. 'I'm not a waiter and I was referring to a cocktail I made up. Here, let me show you. If you don't like it, you can have another on the house.'

Nicole nodded, feeling rather stupid.

'Voilà!' Andy placed a glass in front of her with a flourish.

Nicole lifted the pink-coloured drink to her lips and tested it. 'Fantastic,' she said. 'Sorry about the erm … misunderstanding.'

'No worries,' replied Andy with a wink. 'I like older women and I can recommend it, you know.'

'What?' asked Nicole, gullibly.

'Sex with me.'

Nicole watched, pink-faced as her cocktail, as he moved off to serve another customer. Quickly, she swallowed half the contents of her glass to steady her nerves.

'I can't believe a gorgeous woman like you, doesn't have a boyfriend,' Andy commented a few hours later.

Nicole smiled at him. He had a really sexy voice she decided, maybe she should invite him back that night, she hadn't had sex with anyone other than Darren in the past six years.

'She does,' interrupted a voice.

Nicole swivelled in her stool to face the intruder.

'Why weren't you answering my calls?' thundered Darren, glaring at Andy, his face furious. 'Although now I understand why. Too busy chatting up the local teenagers.'

Andy held up his hands. 'Hey, I'm twenty-three. I didn't know she had a man.'

Nicole shook her head firmly. 'I don't. He slept with my best friend.'

'We need to talk,' Darren lowered his voice, 'I'm really sorry.'

'Don't want to talk.' Nicole sipped her fourth cocktail of the evening and turned away from him.

'Fine,' replied Darren, clearly struggling to curb his frustration. 'I'll be over there when you decide to start acting like a responsible adult.' He stormed to the far end of the bar and pulled out a stool, glaring at Nicole across the bottles and glasses.

Andy raised an eyebrow at Nicole. 'Is he going to be a problem?'

Nicole shrugged and filled him in on yesterday's events. 'So I've cancelled everything, well almost everything. I couldn't speak to the cake artist. I've only dealt with her via email, I do hope she won't charge the full amount. She's probably almost finished it by now.'

'I couldn't help overhearing,' said another voice from beside Nicole. 'I think you should leave it to your idiot ex to deal with.'

Nicole turned to the man standing beside her. He was tall, wearing jeans and a white shirt. His mouth was curled in a half smile and his blue eyes, not dissimilar to Darren's, crinkled at the corners. She instantly hated him.

'I wasn't asking you,' Nicole snapped. 'Another cocktail, Andy.'

'He's just the same you know,' said the stranger.

'What?' asked Nicole sharply.

'The bartender.'

'Same as what?'

'Your ex,' drawled the man smoothly.

'It's nothing to do with you.'

The man shrugged easily. 'Just thought you could do with some advice.'

'And what advice could you give me that could possibly help?' demanded Nicole. 'Andy's helping me fine, thank you.'

'Him?' laughed the stranger. 'He's like that with all the women.'

Nicole glared at him. 'Look, I don't know who you are and I don't care. Leave me alone.'

She watched as the smile dropped from the dark-haired man's face and he turned, his long strides carried him easily to the door. She ignored Darren's mocking laughter from the opposite end of the bar.

A white box was pushed under her nose. 'What's that?' she asked.

'This is a sample of your wedding cake.'

'Are you the idiot I spoke to on the phone earlier?' Nicole asked.

'No,' replied the dark-haired stranger. 'I'm the idiot who made it.'

'But I was dealing with a woman named Kym.'

'I'm Kym but I'm not a woman,' replied Kym, his eyes friendly.

'Darren?' Nicole approached him, on her way to use the toilet.

He looked up at her, his eyes hopeful.

Nicole swiftly dropped the cake on his head. 'You wanted to have your cake and eat it,' she giggled.

From the opposite end of the bar, Kym erupted into laughter.

'Let's go for something to eat,' he called to Nicole.

MOTHER'S DAY VISIT

Barbara Tozer

Nancy felt full of beans, she had so much energy she didn't know what to do with it. 'I will tidy the garage, mow the lawn, clean the windows, dust under the bed, and paint the hall.'

'Hang on a minute,' said a voice that she wasn't expecting to hear. 'You can't do all those things in one day and certainly not all at once, unless you will allow me to help you.'

'But with the best will in the world, how can you help me?' asked Nancy.

'I have friends,' said Bill, 'and they need jobs.'

'Oh,' said Nancy. 'My pockets are not jangling with ready money. I just need to make a start and then you will see that I can manage quite well.'

In the garage Nancy found all manner of unusual objects and she realised that she needed a skip to put them in. Bill told her that environmentally-friendly skips could be obtained.

'Oh are they made of paper?'

'No of course not but what you throw away will be sorted and put to good use.'

Nancy thought that was good for she was beginning to think she had been very wasteful over the years. A paper skip would not accommodate her old lawn mower.

'Do you remember Bill when we needed this roof rack for the people cruiser; we had a car full of your brothers and sisters and all the camping gear. We didn't make it to France but we had a lovely time in Devon.'

'We certainly did and I seem to remember that we lived on baked beans.'

Bill helped Nancy move all the furniture to one side so that she could sweep the dust that had accumulated. She noticed that the mice had been feasting on her armchair. 'Oh that is a shame, my reclining chair will have to go in the skip now.'

'No more reclining for you Mum.'

'No it seems I have a lot of work outstanding. I am beginning to sound like your father,' said Nancy with a giggle.

'Did you say farmer?'

'No but just like a good farmer I must make hay when the sun shines.'

Without the skip to put things in there wasn't much more that could be done in the garage and so they went inside to slake their thirst over a cup of tea.

After tea Bill offered to mow the lawn and Nancy cleaned the windows. It was very satisfying to be able to see through them and out into the street again. She thought the dust must have blown over from the desert again the windows had become so dirty. In the street a bit of commotion was going on. 'Was the rag and bone man out on the streets again? No surely not.' Though in the midst of a recession Nancy didn't think things had become quite that bad. Nancy remembered that as a child a man had come around the streets calling out, 'Rags and bones,' and Nancy would plead with her mother to give the man some fabric, she didn't think her mother had bones, and in return, she would be given a rubber toy, usually something rather gruesome like a snake or a lizard. Anyway the voices disappeared and whatever had caused the disturbance had moved on.

Bill came in from cutting the grass and told her that a group of men had been on the pavement wanting to sell dusters but that a neighbour had dissuaded them saying that this was a no cold calling area.

'That seems rather mean really,' said Nancy. 'I remember when a man came over from France selling onions and people were really pleased to see him. Times really have changed and we do seem rather afraid of our own shadows these days.'

Bill wasn't sure how to reply because it was true people were afraid when strangers came to the door. It was understandable but was it right? Was it harder for people without jobs to be enterprising now or was it more difficult? Bill who was a postal worker wasn't sure. Bill wore a uniform and mostly the people he met were pleased to see him. He knew that for some of his family life had been very difficult. Take his great-great grandfather, he had made a living by collecting wild rose cuttings from hedges and selling them to garden centres! Bill doubted that that would be possible or acceptable now, and perhaps it wasn't then.

'Mum we have done enough work for one day, shall we set the alarm and go out for a little drive in the country?'

'That would be lovely,' said Nancy, 'and we shall nibble some of that lovely dark chocolate you bought me.'

So risking increasing their carbon footprint further with unnecessary travel they both got into Nancy's little Clio and went for a drive through the bluebell woods.

'Just don't be tempted to pick the bluebells,' said Bill. As they sat on a log and contemplated the beauty all around them they felt certain that at least 'The Woodland Trust' should be congratulated for the contribution to everyone's welfare. It was sad but it seemed the man wanting to sell dusters was going to be left permanently out in the cold.

'Time to go home now and sit by the fire,' said Nancy, 'and thank you for a lovely day.'

BATHING ELECTRA

Marion Baraitser

Mary had suggested they go out together that evening but suddenly Rachel started to shout at her, as if some store of pent-up anger had broken loose.

'Why are you so … so … needy? Why must I always be there for you? I'm your daughter for God's sake. Your daughter, not your mother!'

Mary was shocked into silence.

'All this time … since I was five or something - you, you, your every little need … What about me? Why did you never mother me? I needed the mothering, not you!'

'What?'

'Ruined me. With your terrible, terrible need. No childhood. Never allowed to be the child. Always you. Never me.'

'That's ridiculous! I've spent most of life bringing you up, loving you … Seeing to it you had everything.'

'Yes, yes … all that - but underneath, underneath you had this great, black … hole. Nothing inside you. Because your own bloody mother …'

Mary found she could say nothing.

'Love me. Love me! This desperate need of yours … All I wanted … was to be left alone. To grow up.'

'You know nothing. I left my home … My mother … It felt like she'd tied a hand and leg to my back … I thought my breath stank because I was so bad inside.'

'Must you be so bloody graphic!'

'It hurt. And who could I tell? Who would believe me? So I told you.'

Rachel's voice rose higher. 'Yes, me. You never thought about me. Never allowed to be a child! Never! Always there for you. Your needs. Your hurts. How could I survive?'

'Is that what she says, your analyst?'

'It's what I say.'

'They're stupid! Dangerous. They ruin people's lives, analysts!'

A silence lay between them.

'I thought we were friends.'

'You are not my friend. You are my mother!'

Mary sat down as if she had been hit, hard.

A chasm opened beneath her. Rachel, so quick and clever. She had loved her with all her being, from the moment of her birth.

Why was this happening? She would lose her daughter. She became afraid.

'I've got to go,' Rachel said.

'Meet me at the Hampstead Women's Ponds. Your lunch break. We can talk.'

'No.'

'Please. I need to.'

Rachel took up her lecture notes.

'Yes. I really, really hate you,' she said bitterly.

Then she left, banging the door.

Mary went about her household tasks, playing Rachel's outburst over and over in her head. The summer heatwave made the flat stuffy. By lunchtime, the city sweltered in the midday heat, but Mary cycled through Camden as it was the quickest way to get to the Heath. The streets had a feeling of quiet unreality. A storm was in the air.

Sweating, Mary locked her bike at the base of the Heath next to the car park and set her face towards the far corner and the Ladies' Ponds.

She crossed the weedy gravel stretch that begins the Heath, then the bridge separating the Mixed Bathing Ponds from the lake, losing herself in the steady stream of walkers, dogs, children and joggers. A feisty little woman crossed her path. She was bald, one ear was silvered with studs and a diamond pierced her eyebrow. She wore a leather mini skirt and platform shoes. She tugged at the lead of her Labrador that rasped like an old man. How unlike Rachel she was!

Mary veered left up the uneven path in the direction of the old cricket ground, past couples lying almost naked and barely visible in the long, yellowing grass of the slope. Babies toddled over rugs, naked except for sun hats, dogs raced blindly, tongues lolling, wild with the joy of open ground. Discs spun between young men stripped to the waist. Families played cricket, a group of teenagers clapped and sang to the billowing strains of Madonna.

To Mary, everyone seemed absorbed, coping. She felt stripped, blank, but for her memories of sitting there herself, with Rachel.

She crossed the wide tarred path at the foot of the great whispering poplar and she suddenly remembered the sound of the wind like a giant unearthly lyre in a forest of pines on a high hill in Greece when David, her husband of many years standing, told her he was leaving.

The Heath lay before her, a golden-brown lion's pelt caught at the feet of deep green trees and canopied by the brilliant blue sky.

Sweating and panting now (she was none too young and certainly not fit), Mary reached the brow of the hill. The parched Heath spread at her feet like a head of honey-blonde hair shaken out before her, criss-crossed by dark ribbons of pathways and caught by the dark band of water of the Men's Ponds. The scene was serene as a still life.

Something close to a prayer rose in Mary. Let me not have done something so wrong, in my blindness, my ignorance. Let me not have turned my daughter against me.

She did not quite know what to do but began walking again, far too quickly for, suddenly, her foot caught in a pothole and she felt herself crashing forward into the long grass. Helpless, she lay there for a while before heaving herself up. She saw her ankle was beginning to swell slightly. It felt stiff as she put her weight on it.

Anxiously, she dusted down her long skirt and, taking a deep breath, retrieved her sunglasses and cotton hat from the long grass, donned them and walked gingerly down the hill, crossing the next stretch of grassland. A dusky moth flew up at her feet. The trees seemed weary, pregnant with early seed.

Mary limped downhill towards the back gate of the Ladies' Ponds. She passed under the two embracing trees on the brow of the hill, grateful for the momentary shade. Then she crossed the gravel path by the silver birch wood, passed the fenced river of purple willow herb going to seed, and she reached the spot where the old man came on his bicycle to feed the picky, strutting partridge over the fence marking off the pond. Mary pushed open the heavy, spiked gate bearing the notice: The Kenwood Ladies' Pond. No men allowed beyond this point. No children under the age of 12. No dogs.

An enormous sense of relief flooded through her. She thought how often she and Rachel had come here after school to cool off on hot summer afternoons like this one, and wash away the strain of the day. Surely, this was where Rachel would calm down again. This was her space, a haven of peace. Mary slowly walked along the winding, shady gravel path that snaked beneath old trees, pausing when she could first glimpse the waters of the pond, lying like some ancient Greek bathing place. Then she emerged next to the small garden flanking the path on either side, filled with plants given by the women who swam there.

Mary looked anxiously for her daughter but could not see her.

A bird trilled blindly, hidden in the green depths of the thickets of willow and silver birch, reminding Mary that Keats came to this place and heard the nightingale. Mary heard again the nightingale singing one night in Greece when she and David were in bed together, the sound bright in the dark, like liquid amber, flaring the velvet spellbound night, hour after hour of invention, wanton and careless like their love-making. A sudden intense longing for her husband seared her.

Before her, a sea of bodies covered the glade's slope to the water's edge. Mary picked her way carefully between outflung bodies and limbs, piles of clothing, bags, bottles, books and newspapers. Only when she had managed to squeeze herself into a space in the shade at the base of a willow and spread her towel on the ivy-clad roots, did she look around to see if she could spot her daughter. There was no sign of her.

When Mary had wriggled out of her clothes and into her bathing costume, she leaned back and closed her eyes. Scraps of conversation began to dart in and out like small fish or the lines of a Green chorus.

'What did he do?'

'He got up and left.'

'I just want my figure back.'

'Eh alors, je parle avec lui.'

Sweating from the heat, Mary sank anonymously into this mass of unrobed womanhood. After a while, she longed for a cool satiny touch of the muddy water on her skin, though she was a very poor swimmer.

Suddenly she saw the sudden flash of the intense blue of a tiny kingfisher fly across her vision. Then she saw her daughter looking down at her. Mary struggled into a sitting position. Rachel looked away.

'I haven't got much time.'

'Can't we talk?'

'There's nothing to say.'

Barefoot, leaving behind their towels, they made their way across the gritty path to the wooden platform overlooking the muddy water. Rachel saw Mary was limping slightly, but she said nothing.

Her daughter lowered herself down the decaying wooden steps. Bracing herself,

Mary launched into the dark water and doggie-paddled in the direction of the first red buoy. She felt someone clinging to her, then pulling her backwards down into the water's depths, dragging her under the murky water, holding her under. She scrabbled and pushed at the bilious green blanketing her, a blind strength willing her upwards, up, up through the yellow water tomb. Her lungs bursting, she hit the water's surface, gasping for air. Somehow she found herself grabbing an anchored buoy, her legs entangling with the slimy snake-like ropes. Slowly she regained her breath, her strength. Mortified, she looked around for Rachel. Her daughter was nowhere to be seen. Was she imagining things?

Bedraggled, she made her way back to the spot where she had left her towel. Hers was still there, but Rachel's was gone.

Mary dressed. She was in despair. For a moment she was blinded by tears. There was nothing for it but to retrace her steps. Her ankle seemed less swollen. The sun was lower and the trees were beginning to throw their long shadows. The sky was now purple with clouds. She brushed against a giant bed of thistles casting its seed. The deadly nightshade's green berries brushed her skirt as she passed. There was thunder in the air and the sense of the breaking of the drought.

As she limped back up the hill, a sudden thought came to Mary.

'Why am I such a victim - is this what Rachel means? I must learn to be who I like, who I am. Stand on my own two feet. Make myself over, not in Mother's image of me - she needed me to be bad - but in my own image. Swim ... yes, swim, instead of floundering in the shallows clinging to Rachel's back.'

Her heart went out to her daughter.

'I can learn to swim ... Classes at the Swiss Cottage baths for people like me ... Need to learn how to breathe in and out in water. Learn to trust my own arms and legs, to splash and roll and dive like that porpoise I saw once, turning so easily, with such joy in the waves, a jet of blue shouldering the ocean. Yes. Swimming lessons. It's about time. Lost. That's what I've been. Lost in my own terrible needs.'

She would tell Rachel that she was right, make it better between them. She limped on. Drops of rain began to fall. A small bird of prey unexpectedly flew up in front of her. She saw the marbled markings of the underside of its wings and its yellow claws drawn in and its hooded head as it flew strongly up, up into the blue.

UNTITLED

Robert C Barton

Charles Brennan had left Dublin 4 in March that year to come to London to work for his father's brother, Timothy, who had become very successful in the insurance and investment business and had established a large company with a huge turnover. Timmy, as he was known at home, could teach Charlie a lot and help him to success.

It was now autumn, 'the season of mists and mellow fruitfulness'. The nights were drawing in, the warm breezes of summer had gone, replaced by colder winds and more frequent showers. As he left the office that night the winds had stilled and a low damp mist hung over the river, Father Thames.

As the boss' nephew, Charlie was known as Charles, though he had to begin at the bottom of the ladder. Timmy had planned his career thoroughly, like his own. Charles was impatient for success. He was hopeful and was willing to work.

As Charles descended to the street, the sounds of a big busy city met his ears. He pulled up his collar and joined the tapping, scuffling feet of commuters heading for the local station. It was Friday night and Charles was turning over in his mind the events of the day and the fact that he had been invited to Uncle Timmy's for lunch on Sunday.

As he entered the station, Charles checked his watch, realised he needed an evening newspaper and as he stepped briskly towards the ticket collector's gate he saw a paper seller with what was very obviously his very last paper. Charles bought it gratefully. Now he thought he could rest and read comfortably on the thirty-minute train ride homeward.

Charles was relaxed and contented. As Charles sat in the carriage and the fuss and noise of departure had abated, he opened his newspaper.

What happened next was to change life forever for Charles. The newspaper seemed strange - very strange, as Charles discovered. It was next day's paper and the date confirmed it.

Quickly Charles re-checked the date on each page. Yes, it was correct - tomorrow's date. Quickly Charles could see all the financial investment news was there, a day early, also racing results and football results. This could be riches unlimited. He blinked and lit a cigarette.

Quickly, Charles realised that what he held in his two hands could be a sizeable fortune. His training as financial adviser with Uncle Timmy's firm told him that much. He folded the paper and thought and when the train came to his station, he disembarked and went home quickly, to his small apartment. Charles was pensive.

Over lunch on Sunday he said nothing to Uncle Timmy.

Work on Monday was tense and busy. As he went to catch his usual train on Monday - low and behold he met the same paper seller and again he had only one paper left. Charles gratefully bought it again. This time before he came to the ticket collector he glanced at the date. It was the next day's paper again. Charles turned quickly to discover the paper seller had vanished.

That night Charles began to work out a plan to use his extraordinary information and also he still did not tell Uncle Timmy. He began to make investments alone. He made a lot of money.

Two days later he experienced the same paper seller and bought the last paper. Again he vanished. Again it was next day's paper.

He began to collect his paper on a nightly basis now and each time the seller lost himself in the crowd and always the last paper. Charles was convinced Lady Luck was shining brightly on him. No sinister thoughts occurred to him, and he continued now to accrue great wealth on his own. He began his own company. By now summer had arrived again and he became established in many ways to his Uncle Timmy's amazement and who accepted credit for teaching and giving Charles the chance to really become many times more wealthy than he.

Charles was now successful and very wealthy - he had a large house in its own grounds in the country, servants and still he travelled by train and still he bought the last paper from his, by now, mysterious paper seller. He told no one.

Charles continued to become wealthy. He was by now moving in rich and exclusive company. He had a large and energetic staff. Yes, he lived in the country where he had a large house set in its own grounds with swimming pool and tennis court, even a small gym and sauna, a small estate of some twenty acres.

Charles still attended meticulously to his business as Uncle Timmy had taught him. He delegated carefully as he had been taught. His business managers were well chosen as Timmy had taught him. They were energetic and trustworthy yet he alone provided the know how, he alone concealed his information sources, he alone held the ultimate sanction. He alone became singularly very rich and he could pay his staff well. He was a success and also an eligible bachelor.

Charles found time in his busy life to attend functions, social and business. He had many acquaintances and friends. By now he had met and was seen frequently in the company of Kay, the beautiful daughter of the Duke of Molsworth. The Duke was a wealthy banker and property owner. Charles had also become his financial adviser.

Charles and Kay became an item. Romance blossomed and a huge society wedding was planned. A reception at Blandsworth Hall, his country home, and a honeymoon cruise in the Indian Ocean produced and directed by Charles.

He still met his secret, mysterious paper seller regularly each evening.

Charles was meticulous, a planner and by now an astute businessman. Uncle Timmy was proud of him, his family in Ireland were proud of him and he treated them royally.

On his last day in business Charles finished early. He left amid well wishes from his staff. It was now late autumn. The nights were drawing down early and as he left his sumptuous office block, stepping into the early autumn gloom, he thought about how his fortunes had raced ahead in the last year. Yes, Charles admitted to himself, he was keen to succeed and thanks to his secret mysterious paper seller he had arrived almost overnight. He pulled up his velvet coat collar, he still walked to the station though now he was met at his home stop by his chauffeur and rode alone in his Rolls Royce, Silver Shadow, to his country home. He planned to retire early tonight in preparation for tomorrow's wedding. These thoughts ticked over in his head as he approached the steps leading up to the local station to catch his train home.

At the top of the steps Charles was met by his paper seller and as usual only one paper was left, even though Charles was earlier than usual. Charles bought it and at last he thought he would confront his erstwhile oracle, till now and all along, his reason for success. A street vendor yelled close by, someone brushed past him and when Charles regained his stance, his paper seller was gone. Charles did consider it strange, dismissed the thought and continued his journey home.

He suddenly remembered he had not glanced at his newspaper.

When he reached home he left his car and went into the hallway. His footman took his coat and hat.

Charles retrieved his newspaper and went into the living room, where a huge fire blazed. He sat down in his chair near the fire. It was quiet, away from the crowds and noise and rush. Slowly Charles opened his paper to consult prices and investments as usual, but he paused. Tomorrow is my Big Day, he suddenly thought. What are the papers saying? A society wedding, surely they are covering it! What will they say?

He thrust open the front page and was dumbstruck. It said in large black letters - Multi-millionaire bridegroom dies in sleep.

Charles was horrified. Was this the payoff? No happy ever after - nothing?

Charles could not cope. He went to the window; it revealed a starlit night. He called his kitchen and asked for supper and when it arrived he concealed his horror and anxiety. He dismissed his staff for the night and returned to his chair beside the fire. He took his supper slowly, then he slowly lit a cigarette.

He would confront the pay-off. He thought and thought and paced the room. He kicked off his shoes. He paced around for a long, long time.

At last Charles looked at the clock. In the silence of his warm and richly carpeted mansion Charles had just been lost in his thoughts. Time had flown past.

It was 4am in the morning. Charles muttered audibly to himself. 'I have confronted the problem. I will survive. It's 4 o'clock in the morning and I dare not go to sleep ...'

A MOTHER'S LOVE

Shirley Brooks

'Jane, Jane,' the querulous voice of her mother reached Jane as she unloaded the machine of yet another pile of washing; it seemed to have increased to mammoth proportions since her mother had come to live with them three months ago.

'Yes Mother, I'm coming,' she said, trying in vain to keep a note of irritation out of her voice.

'It's eleven o'clock, Jane, time for my morning coffee; and I'll have one of those digestive biscuits - Doctor said I must eat something with my brown pill.'

Jane let the door slam behind her, not bothering to reply; her mind seething with resentment: why didn't her mother get her own coffee for once, she wasn't exactly incapable, but ever since arriving she'd just plonked herself in Ian's chair, expecting Jane to do everything. 'Here's your coffee and biscuit ... now I really must get on, I've a basket of washing to hang out.'

Old Mrs Burdon looked downcast. 'I'm sorry you haven't the time to sit down and have one with me. I'm afraid I make you a lot of extra work ... you should have put me in an old people's home.' Her lower lip trembled and Jane immediately felt guilty.

'Don't be silly, Mum, I can manage. Now who on earth can that be?' Jane said as the front doorbell rang.

She opened the door to find a stranger, an elderly gentleman. 'Mrs Saunders?' Jane nodded. 'I'm sorry to disturb you - my name's Arthur Fulton. I'm an old friend of your mother's, Rose Burdon, I believe she's living with you - I wonder, could I have a word with her please?'

'Will you wait a minute, I'll tell her you're here.'

'Mother, a gentleman is at the door to see you, Arthur Fulton. Claims he's an old friend.'

'Arthur? Arthur Fulton!' she said in delighted surprise. 'Go and ask him to come in right away ... Arthur, after all these years: I can hardly believe it.'

'Would you like to come in?' Jane invited him into the sitting room.

The two old people stood and gazed at each other. 'Rose,' Arthur said, a wealth of emotion in his voice. 'Oh Rose.'

'Can I get you a cup of coffee?' Jane said, suddenly feeling in the way.

'Yes please,' they turned to her in unison.

'Right, I'll go and pop the kettle on and leave you two to get reacquainted.'

'You won't believe this,' Jane said to Ian, that evening, 'Mother's found herself a boyfriend, someone from the past she knew before Dad. He's coming round tomorrow to take her to lunch - she's as excited as a young girl. I've orders to paint her nails and wash and set her hair.'

'Good for her - what's he like?'

'I liked him, he's absolutely charming - obviously nuts about Mum.'

So began a series of regular outings for them and Jane gradually heard the whole story. They had met and fallen in love when her mother was nineteen, and gone out for two years. But Arthur was the only child of a very possessive widowed mother; she hated Rose, as she hated any woman who tried to take her son away. Arthur, torn between the two women he loved, and unable to support two households, had in the end told Rose they must part. Rose then met Jane's father and two years later they married. Arthur had never married, but remained with his mother until she died a few years previously. But he'd never forgotten his beloved Rose, and when fortuitously he met her brother in a local pub and found out she was now a widow, and was living with Jane, he had wasted no time. Now, both in their middle seventies they decided to get married.

After the register office ceremony, Jane's mother took her aside. 'Thank you Jane dear, for looking after me. I know I was a nuisance - I was very depressed and I'm afraid I took it out on you.'

Jane hugged her, tears in her eyes. 'I understand, I'm going to miss you.' And she realised with a pang that this was true.

THE NUMBER SIX BUS

Iris Crew

The number six bus turned the corner and came to a halt. Tom Baker, the driver, was running late, and he wasn't pleased to see several irate passengers waiting to board. Tom had just come from the bus station and his inspector, Mr Patter, had given him a final warning.

The passengers streamed onto the bus in silence, they took one look at Tom's face and thought they'd make the best of a bad job. The number six bus ran from one small town to another and in-between was some beautiful countryside.

It must have been about thirty minutes later when all of a sudden the number six bus came to a stop, and everyone wondered why, they were right in the middle of nowhere, not a house in sight. Tom stood up from his seat and got out of the bus and walked away.

'What's going on, what does he think he is doing?' Harvey Jones, a very big man came from the back of the single decker bus and faced the passengers.

'He must have problems to go off like that, and leave us stranded like this.' Nellie Smith, a quietly spoken elderly lady stood up. 'Perhaps he's having a nervous breakdown.'

'Nervous breakdown or not, he can't just leave us here.' Another man by the name of Fred Martin joined Harvey at the front of the bus.

Carol Hinson almost ran to the driver's seat and sat down. 'Don't worry, leave it to me. It can't be that hard to drive this thing.' She was a small woman of about thirty years of age with bright red hair and the most engaging smile.

'You can't drive a bus without a proper licence.' Harvey looked quite cross to think a bit of a girl like Carol thought she could drive the bus.

'Well, have you got a better idea?' Carol asked Fred and Harvey to sit down. 'Right let's have a go then.'

Carol started the engine and the bus took off along the country lane. Everyone clapped including Harvey who thought now that she was a very brave young woman.

The lane was clear, not a sign of any other traffic. Carol was delighted with this and counted her lucky stars. They hadn't been going long when all of a sudden standing in the middle of the lane, in front of the bus, was Tom, with his head held down.

Harvey again got up from his seat and climbed out of the bus after Carol released the door. 'Now then young man, what do you think you are doing?' Harvey could see Tom was very distressed. 'Is there anything we can do for you?' He put his arm around Tom's shoulder and led him onto the bus.

Tom sat down in the front seat and put his head in his hands, he sobbed. Nellie Smith came over to him and sat down. There was silence throughout the bus, everyone felt sorry for this poor man. Nobody seemed to want to approach Tom except Nellie and, because she was considerate, she didn't force him to talk.

Some minutes passed and the entire bus just sat there looking from one to another, wondering what was going to happen next. Fred stood up and went over to Tom, he asked him if he felt better and did he think he could take charge of the bus once more.

'Please forgive me, something dreadful happened before I left home this morning and to tell you the truth I don't know what is going to happen when I return home.' Tom was obviously distressed.

'Well, let me help you if I can, after all nothing is ever so black as it seems.' Fred was a retired policeman and he was used to giving comfort to the public. 'Would you like some privacy, we could take a walk over that field.'

'I don't know how I am going to explain to anyone what has happened this morning but I know I must talk to someone.' Tom followed Fred off the bus and they walked side by side into the field.

'Maureen, my wife, was diagnosed with cancer two years ago and the treatment went well and she was in remission.' Tom fidgeted about as he talked.

Fred continued to listen and give Tom as much time as was necessary, he thought the passengers were probably a bit impatient by now but decided Tom's needs must outweigh this fact.

'Last week I was driving the bus on this same route and a police car came up from behind me and stopped in front. I thought perhaps the bus had some kind of fault and they had picked it up.' Tom looked at Fred and carried on talking. 'But much to my dismay Maureen had been rushed to hospital, she had apparently fallen down the stairs shortly after I had left for work. My neighbour next door, Sally, calls in around ten o'clock every morning, fortunately she found her.'

Fred assured Tom that he must take his time, although Fred thought, this is going to take forever.

'To cut a long story short, Maureen came home the same day badly bruised but no bones broken, I thought at the time they'd sent her home too soon. Anyway, last night she seemed a little quiet and very tired, she said she had a bad headache. So giving her a hot drink and some tablets to help the headache, she went to bed.' Tom took a deep breath, 'I followed her up shortly after and noticed she was sound asleep. I must have woke with a start around three o'clock and I heard this dreadful noise, it seemed to be coming from the bathroom. Opening the bathroom door, Maureen was lying with her head over the toilet being sick.'

Tom stopped and looked at Fred as if he could help him, but of course Fred could only listen and hope Tom would finally get to the point.

'What happened then?' Fred tried not to sound impatient but this was getting rather absurd. 'Did you call the doctor?'

'No, I managed to get Maureen back to bed and she fell into deep sleep, but about an hour later I was downstairs getting some breakfast because I have to be out early and Maureen started crying out.' Tom paused and the tears ran down his face. 'When I went to her she was gasping her last breath and she died.'

'Now I will take you back to the bus and we will get to our destination. Having done that we will go and see the police. You haven't done anything wrong, Maureen obviously died of natural causes.'

Fred helped Tom onto the bus and asked Carol would she carry on driving the rest of the way.

Fred made sure Tom was seated and Nellie was sitting next to him, then he turned to the rest of the passengers and thanked them for being so patient, assured them that they would be at their destination very soon.

Fred and Harvey sat in a double seat and the rest of the journey Fred put Harvey in the picture. Just in case he needed help to get Tom sorted out at the police station.

Half an hour later the bus reached its end and everyone but Tom, Nellie, Fred and Harvey filed off the bus, patting Tom on the shoulder and saying their goodbyes. It certainly had been an eventful day and one which none of the passengers would ever forget.

The events of the day came to an end when Tom and a policeman, followed by Harvey and Fred, reached Tom's house several hours later, the light in the lounge at the front of the house was blazing. Tom immediately thought this was strange, although he had been slightly disturbed this morning when he had last left the house.

'Tom is that you?' Maureen's voice was unmistakable to Tom. 'You are late.'

'Maureen!' Tom ran into the lounge and there was Maureen lying down on the settee.

'Are you okay?' Tom's face was a picture.

'Yes I am, you went out early this morning, I thought perhaps that you were doing a double shift.'

Maureen then saw the policeman, Harvey and Fred standing there. 'Who are these men, has something happened?'

'I'm very sorry Mrs Baker, there has been an error made, but do not disturb yourself. I'll just have a word in private with Mr Baker and then leave you in peace.'

PC Harrow turned and walked towards the door.

Tom followed him and opened the front door. They went outside and Tom said, 'This is wonderful, Maureen could only have been in a deep sleep after all. I'm very sorry for the trouble I've caused.'

'We are always here to help the public and I for one am delighted with the outcome, let's say no more about it.' PC Harrow got in his car and Tom thanked him for his service.

Tom went inside and explained to Maureen who Harvey and Fred were. He didn't go into details about everything. It would have been stupid to worry Maureen too much. She laughed and thanked Tom's new friends for their help.

They were just as thrilled with the outcome as PC Harrow had been. Tom exchanged telephone numbers with the two of them and they agreed to keep in touch.

MEMORIES NOT FORGOTTEN

Maddie Curtis

Shutting her mobile phone, Jenny stretched out her slender, tanned legs in front of her, resting herself back on her hands. As she sat on the sandy cliff, she closed her eyes and let herself bask in the heat. Her eyes were shaded with designer sunglasses. She tilted her chin towards the sun. A slight breeze sifted through her long blond hair. Bliss, she thought. This is the life.

It was hard to believe this morning she was sitting in the office sending emails and dealing with awkward customers on the telephone, looking out of the window, wishing herself miles away on such a glorious day. Thank goodness for flexi leave. Jenny had left the office and within two hours she was here. She had just left a message on her daughter Anna's mobile telling her to get her own tea.

Anna was at college studying art. It was just the two of them that lived in the flat in a leafy London suburb. Anna, with her artistic flair, had taken it upon herself to decorate the whole flat. It wasn't all bad taste, maybe a little flamboyant in a couple of the rooms, but Jenny had let her put her stamp on it.

The sound beneath her echoed up to where she was resting. She could see excited children and adults paddling and others bobbing up and down in the sea below. People of all different shapes and sizes in their bikinis and swimming costumes. How ridiculous some of them looked - like lobsters, thriving to catch the sun. A speedboat gathered waves, rippling through the water. They are enjoying themselves. That's what it's all about - being here.

Jenny looked to the right of her. In the distance she saw the fair with its waltzers. The Ferris wheel slowly turned and the tracks of the roller coaster with its train on the verge of dipping.

This was Jenny's favourite place - ever since she was eighteen. Her and her friends would come for the day in her Mini Cooper - her pride and joy at the time. Not a care in the world, hanging onto every word the fair people said. Thinking how exciting life would be, living this life, travelling around. The grass was always greener.

How they would make themselves look older with their blue mascara, glossy lipstick and fluffy 'big' hair. Stiletto shoes and ra ra skirts. What tarts we must have looked like. Trying to impress those boys who weren't much older than us.

Jenny gathered her towel and folded it into the straw bag and proceeded to wander down to the bay. A dog obediently ran after the stick its owner threw for it. A father was holding his son's hands trying to fly a kite as it flew higher into the blue sky.

Nearing the pier and seeing the queue wasn't too long, Jenny decided on an ice cream. A small girl stood at the side of the van crying. Having been handed her ice cream it had fallen onto the front of her costume leaving her, eyes closed, mouth open and a shrill to deafen anybody within close proximity. The ice cream seller, feeling generous with all the trade he must have been making today, handed her another one with red sauce dripping all over it.

The beach was swarming with day-trippers, holiday makers, couples walking hand in hand and families and buggies. Jenny sat on the low wall and ate the cool, soft ice cream. Behind her the shops with their stalls of postcards, flip-flops, windbreaks and buckets and spades. The smell of chips wafted across from the burger bar. And Gypsy Rose was still telling people's fortunes where her and her friends had laughed at her predictions. Maybe she would pay her another visit.

How lonely she felt surrounded by all these people.

Ambling along the fairground, the music and business welcomed her. As she wandered amongst the doughnut stand and dodgems she spotted him. He wouldn't recognise her now, not after all this time. Smiling at the customers - girls giggling on the waltzers - using his charm and banter.

Every so often, Jenny had found herself here, on a day trip, escaping from the buzz of city life. Mingling in the crowds she would find him. He still had his good looks. Tall with dark curly hair, although showing a little grey now and the creases in his face appearing as he smiled. Marty was his name. He wouldn't recognise her now.

Life, it appeared had carried on the same for him. He must be the same age as me, a couple of years older maybe. She wondered had he a family of his own now? Were they scattered around the fair. One 'big happy family'? This was the only life he'd known.

Jenny reminisced back to the summer of eighty-eight. Her and her friends had been allowed to stay the week in Tracy's parents' caravan at the camp along Sandy Road. They had visited the fair every evening before her friends went onto the disco - Jazzes. Jenny had made it obvious she only had eyes for Marty. He was charming with piercing blue eyes and a cheery smile that had melted Jenny's heart. Every evening after the fair had closed for the night, they had strolled together along the moonlit shore, his arm around her shoulder, nuzzling her ear. He had been a real romantic or so she thought. They had slept together that last balmy evening. A perfect end to a holiday romance. He had asked her to give up her comfortable life, her friends, her work and family to travel with him and the fairground. His family would look after her.

But Jenny couldn't give up her life for this as much as she felt she had loved Marty. She wouldn't be happy selling candyfloss, tokens for rides or exchanging notes for slot machines.

And so they parted. Two months later she found herself pregnant. Explaining to her parents was hard. They couldn't accept their daughter had fallen in love with someone who she had met on holiday - a travelling boy. How ludicrous. But they eventually did accept their grandchild.

The next time Jenny had driven down to the sea, the fair had packed up for the winter - and become a ghost town. This she knew wasn't the life for her and Marty wasn't to know about Amy. It was a few years after Amy was born Jenny started making her trips to the seaside. Sometimes she would come down on her own and would watch Marty from a distance. If only he knew. Had he really loved her like he said he had?

Now a young lad of about seventeen was working with him on the dodgems. Could it be Marty's son? He had a more slender body but the same curly dark hair and cheeky smile. Amy looked like them. Her hair was dark too but with long curls. And the smile which lit up her face in the same way. You couldn't help but smile back.

Jenny glanced behind her as the noise from the ghost train startled her. At that moment, Marty looked straight ahead and then he saw her. The same girl he had fallen in love with all those years ago. Every so often he noticed her, mingling with the crowd and wondered if she recognised him. He didn't look like the twenty-year-old now who had fallen in love with her back then. She had been different from the other girls he had met. What would my life had been like with Jenny? Yes, that was her name.

Marty was brought back to life with a sudden movement of cars bumping into him. 'Yikes!' he shouted turning one round to face a different direction. A few seconds later, he looked up. She was gone. Not forever - but back to her life - wherever that was.

The weather had been cold, but sunny all week. The month was June and suddenly everything began to pick up and the weather became warmer.

The gardens were looking lovely, roses, marigolds and lupins adorned the scene. The grass was green, and the trees in full leaf.

Everything should have been perfect, apart from one thing, I was alone.

My dear husband had died, my parents were long dead. My three children, brothers, sisters, nieces and nephews all had their own lives. What was I to do? What on earth was I to do?

I tried watching TV, reading books from the library, having days by the sea. I even took a holiday, but came home after three days. I just sat and wept. Every day I got up, did my job, washed and cleaned the house. I had never been really houseproud, but now you could have eaten from the floor. I had gone from the sublime to the ridiculous. I went out every day to the café for a meal, but I didn't even enjoy that and I lost more and more weight as I left more and more food on my plate.

No one appeared to be bothered. One day, I decided what I would do. Yes I would do it! I would look for my loved ones. Suicide was no longer a criminal mental offence. And in any case, what did it matter? I wouldn't be there to listen to it all.

I visited each of my three children in the days up to my departure, they lived locally so it wasn't a problem. I saw my six grandchildren for the last time. No one had any idea of my plans.

I got up early that morning after a reasonably good night's sleep. I washed, dressed and had breakfast. I wrote my note and attached it to the front door above the letter box and stuck it down. I locked the door without even looking back and then I set about my journey.

I caught a bus to the nearest railway station, and then booked a ticket to the town many miles away where I had lived as a child.

The train arrived, I got on and as the train pulled away I had one last look at the area. I just sat and looked out of the window.

Eventually I arrived at my destination and walked away from the main road. I caught a bus to a nearby village and then I walked and walked and walked. It dropped dusk and there was a hotel nearby. Yes I could stay there the night. I was just an ordinary woman with grey hair, no one would recognise me; and in my bag I had the tablets I was going to take. I also had a small bottle of water. I walked until I reached a very secluded spot and then I sat down on the grass. The sun was bright, the birds were singing, a squirrel scampered along the grass, but I knew that what I was doing was right. I felt that my loved ones awaited me.

I took one last look around, and then took my tablets with a good drink of water. I laid back and I waited. I had had one last night in bed.

At home though the story was unfolding. My neighbour had seen my notice which read:- 'I have had enough. I am going to meet my loved ones. All I ask is that the church will give me a Christian burial, according to the Book of Common Prayer'.

My neighbour immediately rang the police and my eldest son. In minutes the house was surrounded by police and they broke in, I had never given my children a key. All there was clean and tidy and there was no sign of me.

The police called the services and a search for me was launched, hospitals and the TV were alerted, but the net was maybe now beginning to close.

A number of people watching TV that evening rang the police and said that they had seen a women fitting my description getting onto a bus. The bus driver also recognised my photograph. My picture and details appeared on the evening news, and the staff at the hotel realised that they had seen me. They phoned TV who notified the police. At that time it appears that everyone from my family, neighbours, the passengers on the bus and the people at the hotel were concerned for my welfare.

At that point the driver of the countryside bus rang the police to tell them where he had dropped me off. Darkness had fallen by this time and the search was called off until daybreak.

It was resumed in the morning and the countryside was awash with searches.

And what about me? I had no idea what was going on, or the trouble I was causing my family. I knew nothing.

My son later told me that everyone was walking in line looking for me, when suddenly a young man walking to one side of the group called out, 'Here!' Everyone rushed to the scene and a policeman, who ran up ahead of the rest of the party, called out, 'I think there's life.'

The police helicopter landed down at my side and the paramedics worked on me. But I can't recall a thing.

I was air-lifted to hospital and for three days I had no idea what was going on. Then suddenly I began to come round. I was very cold and my breathing was bad, however the doctors believed that no long-term damage had been done, and no one else was involved. My family hugged me and I realised that although in recent years they had lived their own lives and I hadn't seen a lot of them, yes I did love them and they loved me. How could I have put them to this worry? In an odd sort of way I was pleased to be alive.

The doctors examined me and said that although I had bled heavily no long-term damage was done. It would be several days before I could eat again, and I would need care and also help to try and get my life together again.

The police were very kind to me, but of course they did have questions to ask me. I had actually wasted police time because I couldn't really prove whether I had intended to take my own life or was it just a cry for help. If so there were people who would have helped me, including the Community Health Care Crisis Team.

After about a week in hospital I was allowed home.

I have been given help and support by the community nurse and a psychiatrist.

I am trying to get back on my feet and have promised my family that I will never do anything like it again.

I have joined a local choir, and a further education class to study history, but maybe the most important thing is that I have started visiting an old people's care home nearby where I meet older people who live there, but don't get many personal visitors.

I have come back from the dead, but my loved ones are still with me.

FORWARD PRESS INFORMATION

We hope you have enjoyed reading these stories
- and that you will continue to enjoy this book in the coming years.

If you are interested in becoming a future New Fiction author, please visit our website, write to us, or give us a call for further information.

This book and other similar titles are available to purchase both through the website and via our customer service line.

NEW FICTION INFORMATION
Remus House
Coltsfoot Drive
Peterborough
PE2 9JX
(01733) 890099
www.forwardpress.co.uk